Meditative Yoga

- integrating body, breath and mind

Meditative Yoga

- integrating body, breath and mind

Are Holen and Torbjørn Hobbel

MOTILAL BANARSIDASS PUBLISHERS
PRIVATE LIMITED • DELHI

First Indian Edition: Delhi, 2012
First Revised English Edition by Dyade Press, 2012
First Norwegian Edition *Yogaboken: Bevegelse og pust*, 2009

ISBN: 978-81-208-3618-1

MOTILAL BANARSIDASS
41 U.A. Bungalow Road, Jawahar Nagar, Delhi 110 007
8 Mahalaxmi Chamber, 22 Bhulabhai Desai Road, Mumbai 400 026
203 Royapettah High Road, Mylapore, Chennai 600 004
236, 9th Main III Block, Jayanagar, Bangaluru 560 011
Sanas Plaza, 1302 Baji Rao Road, Pune 411 002
8 Camac Street, Kolkata 700 017
Ashok Rajpath, Patna 800 004
Chowk, Varanasi 221 001

Cover photo: Karin Malmberg
Book design: Torbjørn Hobbel & Karin Malmberg

All photos of yoga postures were taken by Karin Malmberg at the Acem International Retreat Centre Halvorsbøle. Other photos were taken by people associated with *Acem School of Yoga*, most of them at the following Acem Yoga course venues:

Acem International Retreat Centre Halvorsbøle, Norway
Photos page: 38, 41, 48, 52, 80, 98, 106, 111, 112, 116, 125, 129, 132, 136, 152.

Acem Nordic Retreat Centre Lundsholm, Sweden
Photos page: 24.

The Acem House, Stockholm, Sweden
Photos page: 12, 88, 120, 139.

The Acem House, Oslo, Norway
Photos page: 31, 58.

Acem Meditation retreat in India
Photo page: 148.

This logo belongs to Acem School of Yoga and Norsk Yoga-skole.

ACEM This logo belongs to Acem School of Meditation.

Printed in India
by Aegean Offset Printers
220B, Udyog Kendrea-1, Greater Noida (U.P)
and Published by JP Jain for Motilal Banarsidass Publishers (P) Ltd
41 U.A. Bungalow Road, Jawahar Nagar, Delhi-110 007

CONTENT

FOREWORD

The content of this book reflects Acem's teaching of yoga to thousands of people in many countries over several decades. Our focus on physical yoga is rooted in a meditative tradition. Close to 100 000 people world-wide have learned Acem Meditation, and there has been a growing need for a book that integrates meditative practice into yoga.

For a long time, yoga did not receive much attention in India and Western societies. The growing interest in recent decades has been inspiring, but has not been noted with undivided pleasure. Yoga today is embraced and modified by a number of trendy body disciplines that are quite at odds with its deeper goals. Concerns about such developments have been widely expressed in the question: Is yoga spoiling yoga?

In India, yoga originated in the mists of time and was eventually written down as a classical philosophical system of thought in the *Yoga Sutra*. Physical postures, however, were not known from texts before the 14th century. The bodily postures and breathing practices as we know them today have probably been passed on for centuries in a variety of forms and contexts on the Indian continent. There is no clear lineage of schools or masters. It seems likely that the postures and breathing practices have an inherent strength and effect that have subsisted in spite of changing usage and environments - in the East as well as later in the West. Nevertheless, much of what is taught in yoga schools, health spas and health studios nowadays is quite far removed from classical and meditative yoga. Hopefully, *Meditative Yoga - integrating body, breath and mind* will contribute to a change of direction.

Many people have played a role in the production of this book. Anne Friis-Baastad, a former head of the Acem School of Yoga, and Anne Thomte, the current head, have been untiring in their efforts. We also want to extend our thanks to: Thomas Buch-Anderson, Halvor Eifring, Ole Gjems-Onstad, Maja Grythe, Vilde Drageset Haakensen, Sara Hobbel, Anders Malmberg, Roland Nilsson, Jonas Parandian, Allesandro Ripellino, Giulia Ripellino, Gunnhild Reistad, Ingvill Storli, and Pollyanna von Knorring. Thanks, too, to Vibeke Videm for her help in getting this book translated into English.

Karin Malmberg took the photos of the yoga postures and collaborated with me in creating the book's visual design.

TORBJØRN HOBBEL
SEPTEMBER 2012

Photo: Ole Gjems-Onstad

FOR BODY AND MIND

Over the past hundred years, people's recreational needs have been turned upside down. Formerly, most people's work took the form of physical labour, and they became physically tired and rested in their free time. Nowadays, most of us hold jobs that involve very little physical activity, so we tend to exercise in our spare time. At work, we generally use our brains – our knowledge, social and intellectual skills – to meet the demands of a competitive environment. This means that mental stress is a more prevalent feature of our lives today, and in order to decompress many resort to the unhealthy habit of taking a glass of wine or beer after work. However, there is a growing interest in alternatives, including self-administered techniques like meditation and yoga.

Stress reduction - begin tired, end fit

There is no single medical definition of stress. But we know that in moderate amounts, stress stimulates the organism and is healthy. Prolonged and relentless stress, however, may reduce the mental capacity and be detrimental to physical health. The ideal would be a good balance between stress and relaxation in our lives.

Classical yoga may be of great help in reducing stress and in finding this balance. It comprises physical postures, breathing practices and attention training, also known as meditation. In classical yoga the postures are carried out slowly. Even so, they have significant effects on the inner organs, and on the muscles, joints, tendons and circulation. A person may start a yoga session feeling tired, and end by feeling fit and full of energy. Doing yoga doesn't drain one's energy, but adds to it. Moreover, it produces relaxation, enhances physical well-being and creates a new starting point from which to take on the many challenges in life.

Classical yoga postures make the student freer and more attentive to the body's signals and those in the environment. Practising yoga requires a minimum of space and can be done at any suitable time. It does not presuppose a specific belief or lifestyle, and this independence from ideology and culture has promoted the spread of yoga to all corners of the globe in recent decades.

Silence has many faces.

It may be like the tender love between father, mother and child. It links us to dimensions of existence that are untouched in the clatter of daily life, and bring us peace, contentment and clarity.

Silence may also be frightening, confronting, a reminder of unresolved issues and of a life not lived.

Skiing in Norwegian mountains
- the grandeur of nature.

Photo: Ole Gjems-Onstad

Photo: Karin Malmberg

WHAT IS YOGA?

Our knowledge about the historical Patanjali is limited. Some scholars suggest that several learned men may have written about yoga using the pseudonym of Patanjali. Whatever the truth, Patanjali probably lived about 2000 years ago.

The word "yoga" has several interconnected meanings. Primarily, yoga is a classical Indian philosophical system. It also denotes a number of methods aimed at gaining self-understanding and at providing mental and bodily calm.

In the Western part of the world, most people associate yoga with hatha yoga (body yoga) and pranayama (breathing practices). In a wider perspective, however, yoga encompasses many activities intended to develop awareness and increased capacity for insight. Thus, in the broadest sense, yoga includes physical postures, breathing practices, the cultivation of emotions, thoughts and actions, as well as several approaches to meditation. Meditation is regarded as the most advanced and quintessential form of yoga. In this regard, the intention of yoga is to fulfil the ancient Greek maxim of the Apollo temple in Delphi: "Know thyself."

In addition to philosophy, Indian culture has focused on ways to cultivate consciousness in order to obtain deeper insights into self and existence. Some Western philosophers, for example Pythagoras and his followers in Greece about 2,500 years ago, had a similar orientation. Pythagoras' writings on what he probably considered most important, i.e., lifestyle, diet and insight, are long since lost. Today, Pythagoras is most famous for his mathematical theorem about right-angled triangles.

Yoga sutra

The person credited with writing down the basic doctrines on the philosophy of yoga is called Patanjali. The book *Yoga Sutra* (often translated as "Aphorisms on yoga") was probably written in India about 150-200 AD, maybe 500 years earlier. There are indications that the statements, thoughts and ideas in it had previously existed as oral traditions for thousands of years.

Patanjali's second sutra defines yoga. In Sanskrit it reads:

Yogash chitta vritti nirodhah

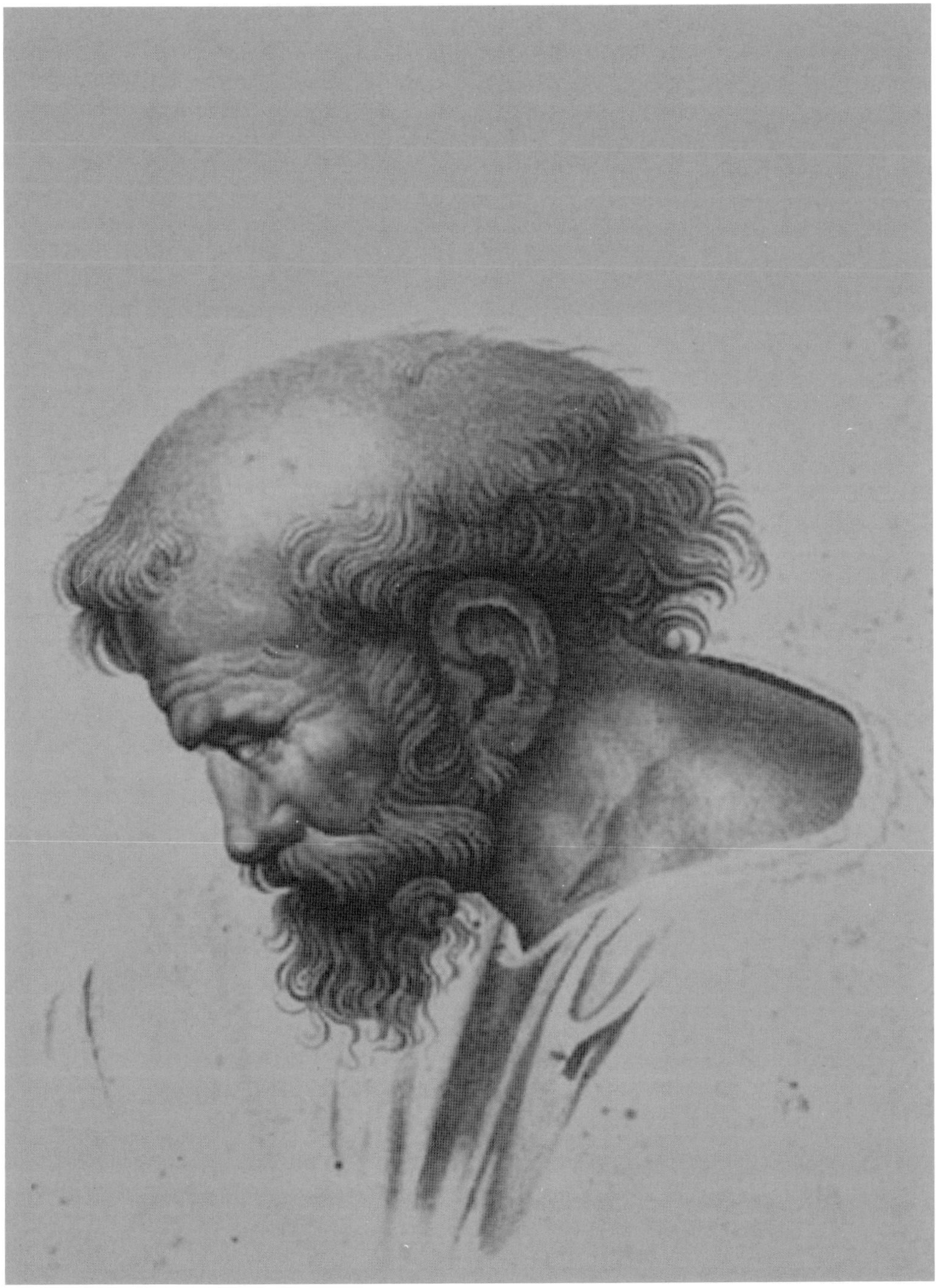

The aphorism "Know thyself" from the Oracle of Delphi is cited by several ancient philosophers, including Socrates and Pythagoras; it underscores humankind's eternal quest for self-knowledge.

Pythagoras of Samos.
Unknown artist

This item may depict a person seated in a meditation posture. It originates from the Indus Valley of Pakistan and probably dates back to around 2500 BC. Perhaps some of the origins of yoga are displayed here?

yogash	– yoga
chitta	– mind
vritti	– fluctuations or activity, incessant changes (may include thoughts, feelings, images, sensations, pain, etc.)
nirodhah	– to silence or annihilate, render calm

Translation: Yoga brings the activities (fluctuations) of the mind to silence.

Meaning of the word yoga: integration

In Sanskrit, the word "yoga" is derived from the root of the verb "yuj". According to *Monier-Williams Sanskrit-English Dictionary*, yuj means to join something together or to assemble something into a whole – for example when attaching a horse to a cart. The word may also mean to make ready, prepare, equip, become absorbed in meditation, become unified or united with the universal, say prayers or perform rites of sacrifice, or to equip oneself with remedies against illness.

In this perspective, yoga aims at helping the individual to become a more complete person through working on one's consciousness. In our opinion, this perspective is the most original and primary aspect of yoga; it covers the classical meaning, i.e., the move towards integration and apprehending the nature of things from within. Integration includes body, breath and mind.

Tradition and transmission

Dating ancient roots and events in Indian history is usually problematic, and this holds true for yoga. Patanjali's *Yoga Sutra* provides a general perspective, but does not describe any yoga practice. The various forms of yoga have emerged over a long time, but it is impossible to ascribe the basic ideas to specific individuals, traditions or eras. Early traces of yoga may be found on some terracotta seals used for trade in the Indus valley in Pakistan, dating from approximately 2,500 BC or earlier. They display people in postures suitable for meditation. However, the script on the seals has so far not been deciphered, and it is therefore unclear what the figures allude to.

A few written works on physical yoga from the 14th century and later are preserved, but they are unsuitable as textbooks. In addition, they contain elements from other traditions, and the body yoga they describe is very different from yoga as we know it today. There also exist a few manuscripts with illustrations of yoga postures from the beginning of the 19th century. On the whole, rather than being codified in writing, physical yoga has been passed down from masters to students over the centuries.

This book is built on Patanjali's definition of yoga. This means it is based on the principle of a free mental attitude with the aim of self-realization. It involves working with the physical foundations of our existence, our thinking and feeling, our perceptions, decisions and actions.

Different approaches

It is often said that yoga is based on traditions from thousands of years back, as if yoga were one unified tradition. This is not true. There are several, widely varying ways of performing the postures. This diversity shows some of the flexibility and adaptability of yoga, but it may also have contributed to diluting the content.

Somewhat freely, we have translated hatha yoga as physical yoga or body yoga. In Sanskrit, hatha means power, discipline or strength. Hatha yoga implies using discipline to achieve a mastery of the various physical postures. Body and mind are endowed with power and strength.

In a later text on yoga, *Hatha yoga pradipika*, from about 1350 AD, the use of ascetic self-discipline or even self-torture is mentioned. Such perspectives do not belong to the main branches of hatha yoga, and they are therefore not pursued in this book. We build on Patanjali's definition and the principle of a free mental attitude. In any kind of yoga, the ultimate aim is self-realization, and in hatha yoga this is achieved by cultivating the physical basis for consciousness.

Yoga comes to the West

Since the era of Romanticism at the end of the 18th century, some people in Europe and North America have looked to India for inspiration and under-

The picture to the right shows a page from a manuscript on physical yoga from the 19th century, purportedly by a Maharaja of Mysore in South India. The illustrations do not always make it easy to understand the intended postures and movements.

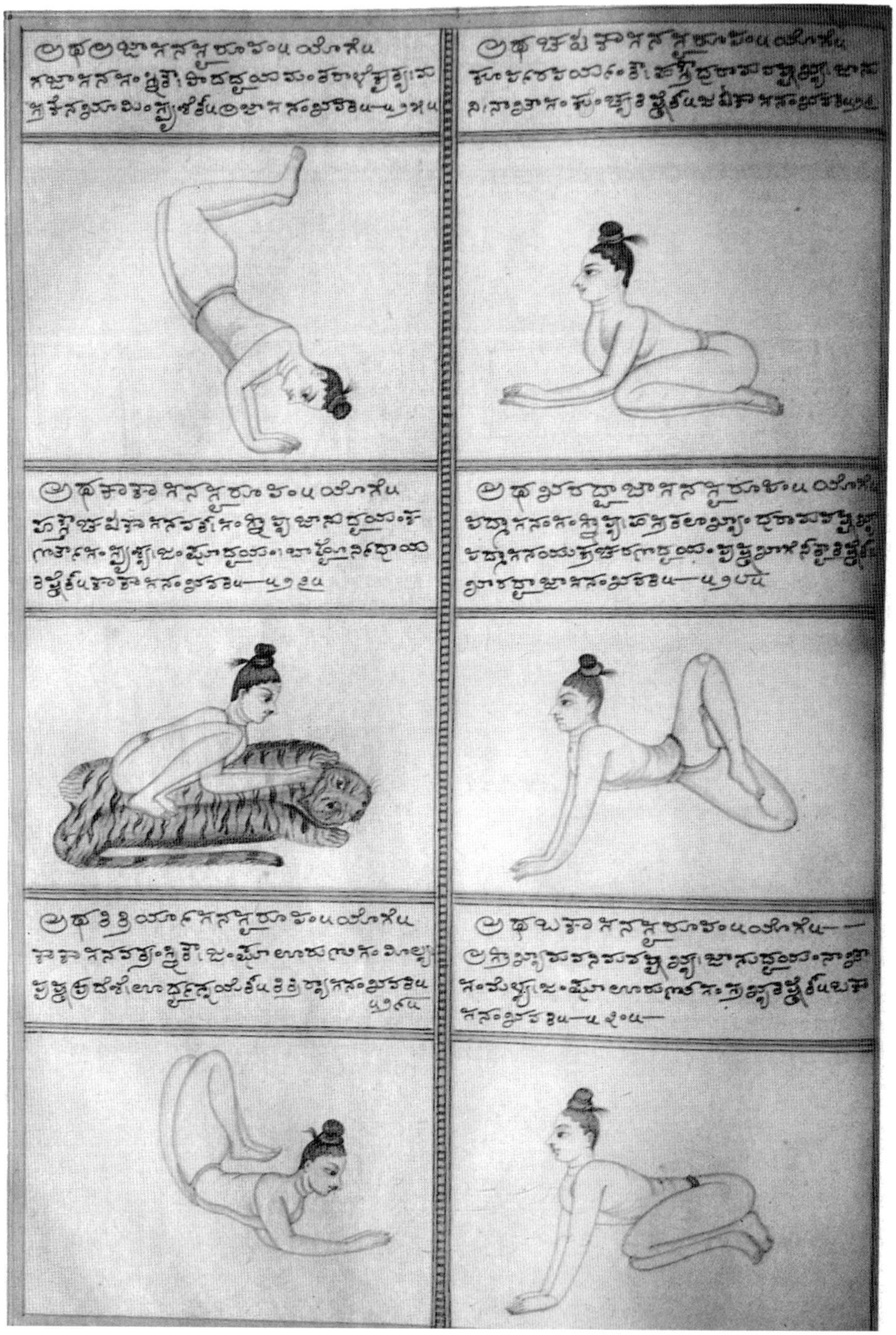

standing about the deeper aspects of existence. The widespread Western interest in yoga emerged much later, in the 1970s and even more strongly in the 1990s. Acem School of Yoga was founded before the first major wave of yoga in the West.

Alain Daniélou, a French professor at the BHU – Benares Hindu University in Varanasi – published a thorough and impressive exposition of yoga in 1949. It is not a textbook, but an account of central aims, ideas and concepts with a large number of references to classical Sanskrit texts. The title of the book is *Yoga – The Method of Reintegration*, which is meant to explain the meaning of yoga. In classical yoga, however, "reintegration" is never an issue. The word reflects a European idea about a "Paradise lost" which is without Oriental roots. In yoga, one is not trying to reachieve a lost state of childlike integration, purity or innocence. Instead, one is attempting to reach a state that has never previously been attained. Achieving this requires persistence and mobilization of the inner resources of the mature, reflecting adult.

Yoga gymnastics

Yoga has been disseminated in the West through many different channels. Much of what is currently taught in yoga classes and displayed in magazines, books and DVDs about yoga represents an odd mixture of Eastern and Western approaches to fitness and training. Let us also add that in our opinion, it is not necessarily a mark of quality today that the teachings have an Indian basis.

A sort of synthesis between Indian yoga, English calisthenics and martial arts was developed in the palaces of the maharajas of Mysore in South India during the nineteenth and twentieth centuries, especially from the middle of the 1930s. The result was various types of yoga gymnastics aimed at providing physical and mental training for the royal princes. B.K.S. Iyengar and Pattabhi Jois (the father of ashtanga yoga) were prominent figures in this movement. Pilates also seems to have similar origins. Such teaching revolves around intense exercises that increase the heart rate, circulation and breathing in ways that are incompatible with meditation, silence and insight. This form of yoga

Krishnamacharya was the teacher of B.K.S. Iyengar, Pattabhi Jois and others. He was inspired by British gymnastics or calisthenics. In this photo, he is teaching the pupils by standing on the abdomen of a young boy in the bow pose.

characterizes much of what is presently taught, in India as well as in the rest of the world. Our exposition covers an entirely different orientation.

In this book, the words "pose" and "posture" are used interchangeably to cover the Sanskrit word "asana". We have deliberately avoided using the word "exercise" as it is closely associated with gymnastics and sports, and it thereby signifies something remote from the meditative qualities of yoga that we want to underscore.

Classical or meditative yoga

This book follows a meditative, classical approach to yoga. The aim is silence in the mind, *chitta vritti nirodhah*, in other words, bringing the activity of the mind to rest and peace. This is in accordance with Patanjali's definition.

The postures described in these pages are conducive to health, fitness and deeper meditation practices such as Acem Meditation and certain kinds of mindfulness meditation. Classical yoga of this type is useful for anyone who wants to unwind, be re-energised for the challenges of life and acquire self-insight. This sort of yoga strengthens both body and mind in more comprehensive ways than yoga gymnastics.

Some exceptions

This book also includes a few practices that do not originate from what may be considered as classical or meditative yoga.

Surya namaskar, salute to the sun, is not a classical yoga posture. It was developed in Southern India in recent times, and it was first taught in our context in the early 1960s by India's ambassador to Norway, son of a former Maharaja of Mysore. The value of the exercise lies in its powerful stimulation of the circulation and muscles, and it should be thought of as a kind of yoga gymnastics.

The impulse practice is inspired by parts of the Tantric traditions. It has been included because it may enhance the practitioner's contact with unresolved inner psychological issues and bring relief. It is not part of classical yoga, but we consider it useful for its potential to open inner aspects of the psyche that may be cultivated further by classical yoga and meditation.

Basic distinctions in yoga and meditation

In the book *Acem Meditation: An Introductory Companion* (Acem Publishing, 2007), Are Holen writes as follows:

> One of the most essential distinctions between meditation practices [is] the difference between what we may call (1) directed techniques (or concentration techniques), which tend to be strongly state oriented, and (2) non-directed techniques, which tend to be process oriented. ... In concentration techniques, the point is to stand porter at the entrance of the mind and allow nothing undesirable to get in. Often the goal is to get rid of all thoughts. (Page 51)

He continues:

> In non-directed techniques [however] the mind's spontaneous activity is a central element of the meditation. Rather than suppressing this stream of consciousness, the aim is to gain access to it by relaxing control. At the interface between the willed and involuntary activities, by relaxing the breath and/or allowing the free flow of consciousness, the student may enter fascinating and revitalizing areas of the psyche. Only a non-directed approach enables work with the unconscious. Goal orientation has a tendency to interfere with these processes.

A similar distinction applies in yoga. To a large extent, the outcome is related to the attitude adopted by the student in the performance of the postures. In yoga gymnastics, force, speed and concentration are often applied. The approach emphasized in this book is in the opposite direction; it is characterized by softness, calmness and a free mental attitude. The point is not to discipline the body and mind by force, but to find the coordinated flow in movements and breath, and to open the mind to awareness of the body and the spontaneous stream of consciousness. In this way, the student may work through issues of the body and mind. Free mental openness allows silent aspects of existence access into our lives.

Are Holen founded the Acem School of Yoga in 1968, at the age of 23. At that time, he had been practising and teaching yoga and meditation for several years.

This is from a yoga class led by Are Holen in 1970.

An article in the weekend magazine of the leading Norwegian newspaper, *Aftenposten*, covered the Acem School of Yoga and published this photo.

Photo: Roland Nilsson

PRINCIPLES OF YOGA PRACTICE

There is no competition in yoga. Every person progresses at his own speed, in his own way. Regular practice over time brings gradual improvements. There is no rush towards ever new goals.

Only patience and persistence pay off in the long run.

There is no competition in yoga. The underlying principle is a free mental attitude. Each person starts from where he or she is, takes the time required and awaits progress without impatience. This section outlines the basic principles of physical yoga as taught in this book.

1. Stretch

In the yoga postures, the muscles are to be stretched gently. When the point of maximum stretch is reached, the stretch should be maintained for 30-60 seconds without causing strain or pain in the breath or body. When regularly stretched, the muscle fibres and tendons gradually respond by changing their tonus and elongating slightly.

Careful stretching is compatible with calm, unrestrained breathing and flow in the body movements. What happens in the muscles during stretching is similar to what occurs during relaxation. Stretching too far, however, will provoke pain, and the breath and the body movements will lose their gracefulness. This indicates that the person is pushing himself too far.

In sports and gymnastics, the main emphasis is on muscle contractions involving force, while in yoga the main emphasis is on stretch, but always within limits that fall short of binding the breath and movements.

2. Differentiated and coordinated movements

Done properly, yoga entails very little expenditure of energy. However, a beginner tends to use far more muscles than required, and also to struggle and strain. For example, when moving the back in unfamiliar ways, the facial muscles may be involuntarily contorted, the breath constrained, the legs or bottom tightened, and so on. With more practice, only the necessary muscles are involved. Such improvements are called differentiation and coordination; they come with practice and develop more quickly when also the attention is used - as described in paragraph 6 below.

3. Slow pace

In classical yoga, movements should be slow and should be made at a constant, unhurried pace, without force, jerking or pulling. The same goes for the transition from one posture to the next. The principle of slow movements is not applicable to the sun salutation (surya namaskar, page 96) or the impulse practices (page 107).

4. Half-open or closed eyes

When more experienced, it is advantageous to do yoga with half-open or even closed eyes. In this way, the student becomes more aware of the inner aspects of the movements, breath and mind.

5. Breathing through the nose

During the practice of yoga, it is preferable to breathe through the nose. Under times of stress or strenuous physical exercise we tend to breath through the mouth to supply the tissues with enough oxygen. However, when we have an inner focus associated with rest, calm and meditation, we normally breathe through the nose.

6. Coordinating breath and movement

The yoga postures should be done together with deep, calm and regular breathing. The full yoga breathing (page 124) is frequently used. This manner of breathing will be audible to the student from inside of the body. The sound usually comes from the back of the nose or the throat.

The pace of the physical movements should be attuned to the rhythm of the breath. We might say that the breathing controls the movements, and the movements control the breathing. For instance, when bending forward, it is natural to breathe out. When lifting the arms, the ribs are lifted too, so it is natural to breathe in. Movements should be synchronized with the breath so that, for instance, breathing in does not start or end before the body movements start or end.

Rosewater
Photo: Karin Malmberg

7. Use of attention

Before students of yoga have mastered a posture, most of their attention will be directed towards the physical movements. With increasing capability, the attention should be directed towards the manner of breathing whilst doing yoga. Later on, the attention is used to enter deeper into the meditative mode.

Attention to movements

With regular practice, the body will readily adapt to the yoga poses. The slow pace allows the attention to observe closely every aspect of the movements. In this way, the student becomes aware of undifferentiated use of muscles, the tendency to use force, to move without coordinating the breath with the movements, and any binding of the breath. By focusing the attention gently, the quality of the movements gradually improves.

When practising yoga, the attention should gently observe the movements, postures and breathing with a free mental attitude, in an undirected yet attentive manner.

Breathing

As the quality of the movements improve, more attention may be given to breathing. The movements should be well coordinated with the breath and vice versa. The breath should then be observed whilst it is going in and out. In particular, the student should be aware of and avoid any tendencies towards restricting the breath. Gradually, the work on unrestrained breathing will bear fruit, and the breath will flow in and out quite freely – even in the more complicated postures.

A guiding principle is to let the free, unrestrained breathing decide how far into the postures a student goes. When trying to adopt a pose that one is not supple enough to manage fully, the muscles tend to respond by tensing as a protective measure, and the breath becomes restricted. At that moment, if the breath is made more relaxed, the body may slowly let itself move further into the pose without resistance.

The attention should be directed both from the outside and from within the body.

From the outside the student follows the movements with the eyes, observing the outermost parts of the body in motion whenever possible. For example, when lifting the right arm, the eyes may be resting on the hand as it slowly moves upwards. The gaze should not be concentrated or intense, but broad in its perspective so that the entire body is taken by a "wide angle", and simultaneously, the student is aware of the movements in body and breath. To begin with, the eyes may be used, but with more practice the observation may be done with eyes partly or entirely closed, so that the student is watching with the "inner eye".

In classical yoga, not one single posture but a sequence of postures is important for building up the potential for deep meditation at the end.

From within implies awareness of how the movements are felt from inside the body: which muscles are strained, how the breath is restricted, which tendons are being pulled unnecessarily or what may feel uncomfortable.

Meditative mode

As the student gradually begins to unite breath and movement in the postures, it is time to adopt a more meditative approach, using an unfocused awareness of the entire body. The attention should be free floating and undirected, so that it encompasses all this at the same time in an unstrained manner. This meditative mode, a free mental attitude, is reinforced by keeping the eyes half-open or even completely closed at times. In this way, there is a degree of convergence between the mindset involved in performing a sequence of postures and the corpse pose (sava asana, page 114) towards the end.

8. Mobilization and relaxation

Yoga involves frequent changes between mobilization and relaxation, i.e., between moving and holding a pose, on the one hand, and relaxing after the postures, on the other. In these alternations lies an important element of training: the ability to shift and adapt swiftly between the opposing demands of using the muscles and relaxing them. The change towards relaxation is made when we lie down after postures and "let go of everything" for up to 30 seconds, before we flex our muscles again and start the next posture.

9. Ending the sequence with the corpse pose

In classical yoga, not only each individual posture, but also the whole sequence of postures is important in building up the potential for deep meditation at the end. The climax is reached in the final corpse pose. Here the mind is allowed to flow freely for some minutes; it usually goes into a spontaneous meditative dive that further vitalizes both mind and body.

Photo: Ole Gjems-Onstad

Photo: K

MOVEMENTS
OF BACK AND UPPER BODY

Musculoskeletal problems are frequent causes of discomfort, sick leave and disease.

In modern sedentary working life, parts of the spinal column are often overused while other parts are not used much. This imbalance may make some areas of the spine too lax and other parts stiffer than is desirable. By using the principles below, this imbalance can be corrected. Different sections of the back have varying degrees of flexibility and motility.

Many yoga postures involve forward and backward movements of the back and the upper body. In some detail, we will describe below how the back should be moved in the postures when

- bending forward
- bending backward
- rotating

Forward flexion of back and upper body

Bending the body forward consists of two steps. The movement should start from the hips, producing a slight inward arching (belly out) of the lower back. Gradually, this inward arch should move up along the spine until it reaches the area between the shoulder blades or scapulae, continuing further up along the line made by the shoulders, neck and head. The first step ends about half-way down at a point when the whole back, shoulders, neck and head are involved in the inward arch.

When this half-way point is reached, the second stage begins. This involves an outward bending (belly in) that also starts in the lower back and gradually moves upward so that the back is curved towards the body from the lower to the upper parts. Finally, the shoulders, neck and head are flexed outwards, too.

To sum up, when bending forward, the back is subject to two major movements: first, a slight inward arch (belly out) and then an outward arch (belly in). In both phases, the movements should start from the hips and gradually spread upwards.

Going back up can be done in two ways – with or without arching inward from the hips.

1. *Without arching:* The upward movement is started by first pressing the chin towards the neck. At the same time, an outward movement of the spine starts from the hips and rolls up along the spine until the

Photo: Karin Malmberg

Yoga makes it easier to accept the imperfections of the body. There is no contradiction between improving and accepting physical defects. An open mental attitude facilitates both. In postures requiring flexibility and precision, an attitude that is not focused on achievement gives the best results.

From the periodical Dyade no. 1-1995

back becomes upright. Finally, the chin is lifted; this marks the end of the upward movement.

2. *With arching (more difficult):* The movement starts in the lower back. By making an inward tilt in the lumbar region, the upper body is almost lifted upward. Slowly, let that inward arch move upward along the spine until it reaches the shoulders and neck. When the back has been lifted about half-way up, continue upward by gradually reducing the arching of the back. Begin with the lower back, and continue along the spine until the movement is completed and the back is straight.

Backward flexion of back and upper body

In the yoga postures that include a backward flexion of the upper body, the movements usually start from the head, and it is essential that the head "governs" the movements. The head is curved backward, initiating a slight inward curving in the upper parts of the back (chest out). Let the top point of the curve move down along the spine from the neck to between the shoulder blades, down to the lower back (lumbar region), and finally to the hips. The flexion should take place as a smooth, gradual movement through the entire spinal column.

When returning to the starting position, the movements are again to begin from the hips by arching the lower back inwards (belly out). This arch should then move upwards along the spine until it passes the area between the shoulder blades. The head and the neck are the last parts to be lifted.

Twisting the upper body

In some yoga postures the torso is twisted. The full effect of the twist is achieved when the student is capable of keeping the spinal column relatively straight in the postures. This may be difficult at the beginner's level, when a simpler variety of the twist posture is recommended. It is possible to make a limited and careful twist with a slightly curved spine.

Photo: Roland Nilsson

Photo: Torbjørn Hobbel

ADVICE FOR YOGA STUDENTS

Every person has to find a way of practising yoga which fits their daily routine and accords with their preferences and interests.

What time of day?

The morning is recommended as the best time for yoga. The body is stiffer then, but aided by yoga, it becomes freer and suppler for the rest of the day. Experience also shows that many people benefit from doing yoga after work and at night. If it cannot be done at these times, any convenient time will do.

Meals

Yoga is best done on an empty stomach. If the postures are to be performed after a heavy meal, preferably wait 1.5–2 hours before starting. After a lighter meal, the waiting time may be shorter.

Environment

It is preferable to do yoga in quiet surroundings, and in a well lit and well ventilated room.

Yoga mat

Do yoga on a surface that is not too hard or too soft. A mat or a rug will serve the purpose well.

Clothing

Yoga is best done in loose garments that will not inhibit movement or breathing. Avoid anything tight around the neck, chest, abdomen or legs.

Shower and bath

In the morning, it is recommended to take a quick bath or shower before yoga.

Photo: Karin Malmberg

Frequent or sporadic practice

As with all mental or physical training, regular practice of yoga over time gives the best results, even though single sessions are rewarding. Every person has to find a way of practising yoga which suits his time, opportunity, liking and interest.

Yoga and meditation

Meditative physical yoga and meditation go very well together. We recommend doing meditation immediately after a yoga session, if possible, as this is likely to lead to better and deeper meditations. In this case, the final corpse pose may be kept short, only 3-5 minutes, or it may be skipped completely.

Yoga and meditation combine well with an active, modern lifestyle and enhance overall well-being. The time spent on yoga is repaid in the form of more energy, higher stress tolerance and a sharper focus of attention.

Photo: Ole Gjems-Onstad

Many people wonder whether to choose yoga or meditation. The answer depends on individual interests, preferences and objectives. If stress management and a supple body are the highest priorities, yoga is the right choice. If the interest is in personality development and psychological insights, Acem Meditation is more suitable. Practising yoga postures hardly leads to deeper personality changes, but it does enhance well-being. The combination of yoga and meditation yields more benefits than either of the two separately.

Those wanting to learn meditation probably already know that there are a lot of approaches on offer, but they are far from equally good and effective. So consider carefully before making a choice. Schools that offer numerous meditation techniques for various purposes are usually not good quality. Based on experience, we advise avoiding mood-focused meditations with an emphasis on "feeling good", extraordinary experiences, altered states of mind or powerful emotions. Scientific measurements of the physiological changes taking place during such kinds of meditation have demonstrated that there is often very little effect.

Ideally, go for a form of meditation that is not based on concentration. Non-directive methods seem to work far better. A useful criterion is that the method has well-documented physiological effects towards relaxation. We recommend Acem Meditation, certain forms of vipassana, zen or mindfulness meditation. Some kinds of meditation may be learnt from books or CDs, but those who are serious in their pursuit are recommended to find personal instruction and guidance along the way.

Anyone wanting to start meditating regularly should opt for one of the more profound methods. Two criteria to check when choosing a meditation technique: that it has well-documented physiological effects towards relaxation, and that the teaching is not part of a person-centred cult.

Yoga and diet

Practising yoga is compatible with any healthy and well-balanced diet, although a lacto-vegetarian diet may sometimes be advantageous. Try to eat regularly and not too much.

Those inclined to modify their lifestyle might consider avoiding tobacco, coffee, tea, alcohol and illegal drugs. Onion, garlic, leeks and chives also inhibit some of the physical and mental abilities for going deeper in yoga or meditation. The effects of such foods may last up to 36 hours after intake.

Photo: Ole Gjems-Onstad

PATTERNS OF YOGA POSTURES

Lack of flexibility, stiff joints, weak muscular control and poor bodily comportment are sometimes the physical manifestations of inner conflicts. Yoga works on the physical expressions of such conflicts, and makes the underlying psychological issues more available for modification.

FROM THE PERIODICAL DYADE
NO. 1-1995

Each posture in this book follows the same pattern: *starting pose – into the pose – hold the pose – out of the pose – rest and relax*. The descriptions usually follow this pattern step by step.

1. Starting pose

Each yoga posture begins with one of several starting poses. These are described in a separate chapter (page 49). The postures also end in the starting pose.

Before going into a posture, take 2-3 full yoga breaths. This can be done lying down or in any other starting pose.

2. Into the pose

From the starting pose, slowly and smoothly move into the posture. The movements should be coordinated with deep and calm breathing – in and out. Let the attention register every aspect of the muscular movements and the manner of breathing. In this way, the student becomes increasingly aware of how to integrate the body, the breath and the mind.

3. Hold the pose

When the process of moving into the posture is completed, the position should be held for a little while. The body should be quiet and the mind at rest. Usually, the student observes his free and relaxed breathing. This constitutes one of two meditative parts of the postures.

For beginners, the pose may be held for approximately 5-10 seconds. With more practice, the duration may gradually increase up to 30-60 seconds. Experienced students may hold the position even longer without effort, but generally we recommend that a posture should be repeated two or three times instead. By repeating a posture, the static and dynamic elements of yoga are combined in a balanced way.

The beginner should mainly let the attention rest on the body to improve the quality of the performance. When the use of the muscles is reasonably well mastered, the range of attention should be extended to include the breath and the bodily sensations that may accompany the pose. Later on, the attention should take in everything with a meditative, unfocused awareness. At that time, breathing should not be directed, but should flow freely with an open, restful, observing attitude.

4. Out of the pose

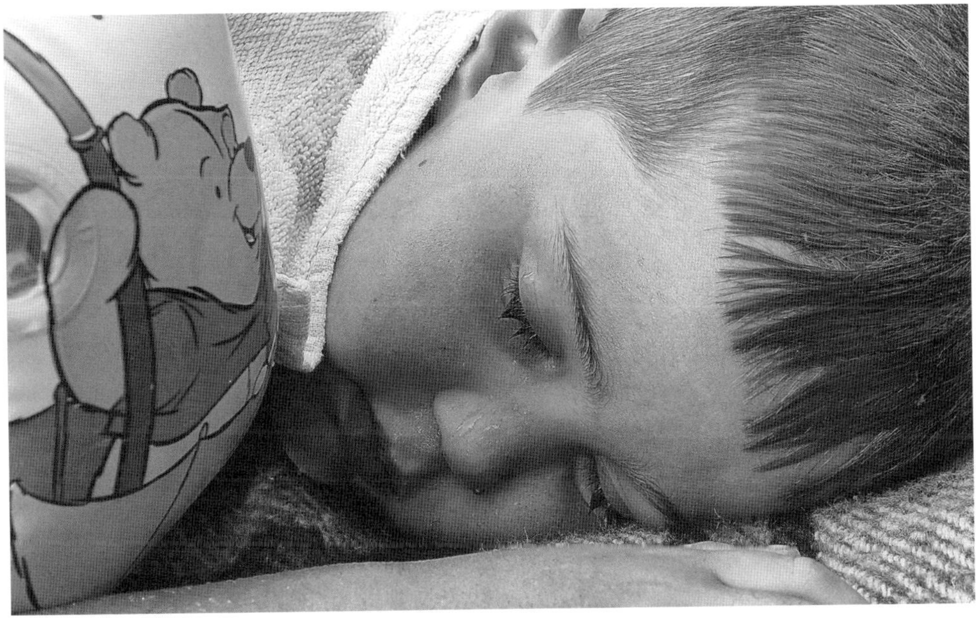

Photo: Karin Malmberg

After holding the posture, slowly move out of it and back into the starting pose. Once again the movements should be slow and synchronized with deep breathing. The attention observes the slow movements and the breath from both within and without. Thus, the student is aware in an unfocused manner of the breath, the movements and the sensations in the body - from the moment of starting until the moment of completing the posture.

5. Rest and relax

After finishing every posture, the student may remain in the starting pose or lie down for a short while. This short rest constitutes the most meditative phase of a posture, while holding the pose is the second most meditative phase. During the short rest, the yoga student should let go of all residues or tensions caused by doing the posture. The attention should be free floating rather than observant. In other words, the rest and relaxation stage involves an undirected, spontaneous flow of the mind.

The resting periods should not be long, no more than 30-45 seconds – a time frame just sufficient for the body to calm down. After this short rest, take 2-3 full yoga breaths before moving into the next pose.

As the sequence of postures proceeds, the physiological potential for going deep into meditation between postures increases. The student should resist taking longer rests between postures, instead saving the deep meditation for the end of the sequence in the corpse pose (page 114).

Photo: Karin Malmberg

STARTING POSTURES

Starting poses

Every yoga posture begins and ends with a starting pose.

Sitting on the heels

Kneel down with the feet tucked under the bottom. Place one of the big toes on top of the other and twist the heels slightly outward. Sit down on the heels. Place one hand in the other with the palms up. Keep the back naturally straight. PICTURE 1

Sitting cross legged

Sit with the legs crossed. Shift your body weight slightly forward and sit on the sitting bones, not on the tail bone. Place one hand in the other, palms up. Keep the back naturally straight. There are different versions of this starting pose. PICTURE 2

Sitting with straight legs

Sit with the legs extended straight in front of you and parallel to each other. Place one hand in the other with the palms up. Keep the back naturally straight. The knees may be bent slightly. PICTURE 3

Lying on the stomach

Lie on the stomach with the forehead facing down and the arms extended along the sides. The inner edges of the feet should touch each other. When ending certain yoga postures, you can rest with one cheek on the ground, alternating sides each time the posture is completed. PICTURE 4

Lying on the back

Lie on the back with the arms along the side of the body and the palms facing upwards. The inner edges of the feet should preferably touch each other. PICTURE 5

Standing with the feet together

Stand with the feet approximately a handbreadth apart. The soles should rest firmly on the ground and the body weight should be equally distributed. Let the arms hang straight down. PICTURE 6

Starting poses

PICTURE 1

PICTURE 2

PICTURE 3

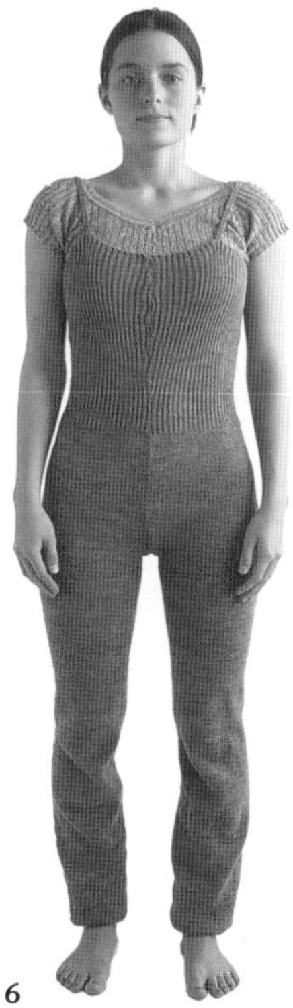

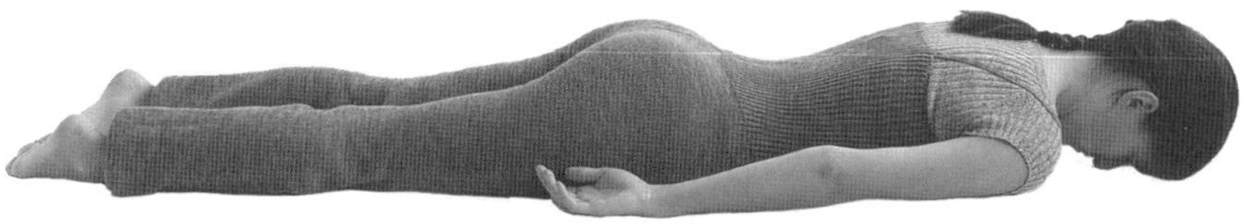

PICTURE 4

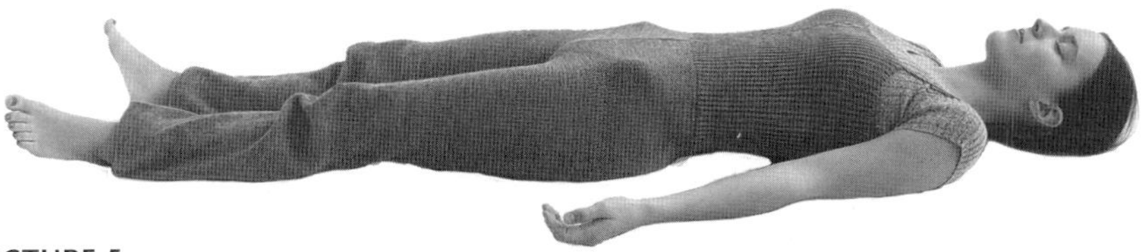

PICTURE 5

PICTURE 6

Photo: Ole Gjems-Onstad

INVERTED POSTURES

Low shoulderstand

viparita karani

Starting pose

1 Lie on the back with the arms along the sides.

Into the pose

2 While breathing out, keep both legs extended and lift them and then the hips up from the ground to form a 90° angle between the back and legs.

3 Support the hips with the hands.

4 Find the balance.

5 Keep the knees straight and the ankles and toes extended during the entire pose.

Hold

6 In the beginning, hold the pose up to 15-30 seconds. Gradually increase to 60 seconds. Relax all muscles that are not required to hold the pose. Observe free and relaxed breathing.

Out

7 While breathing out, keep the legs straight and lower them towards the face. At the same time, place the hands on the ground, palms down.

8 While breathing in, return to the starting pose by lowering the hips and letting the extended legs follow slowly.

9 Lie on the back to rest.

Easier version:
Bend the legs when going into and out of the pose.

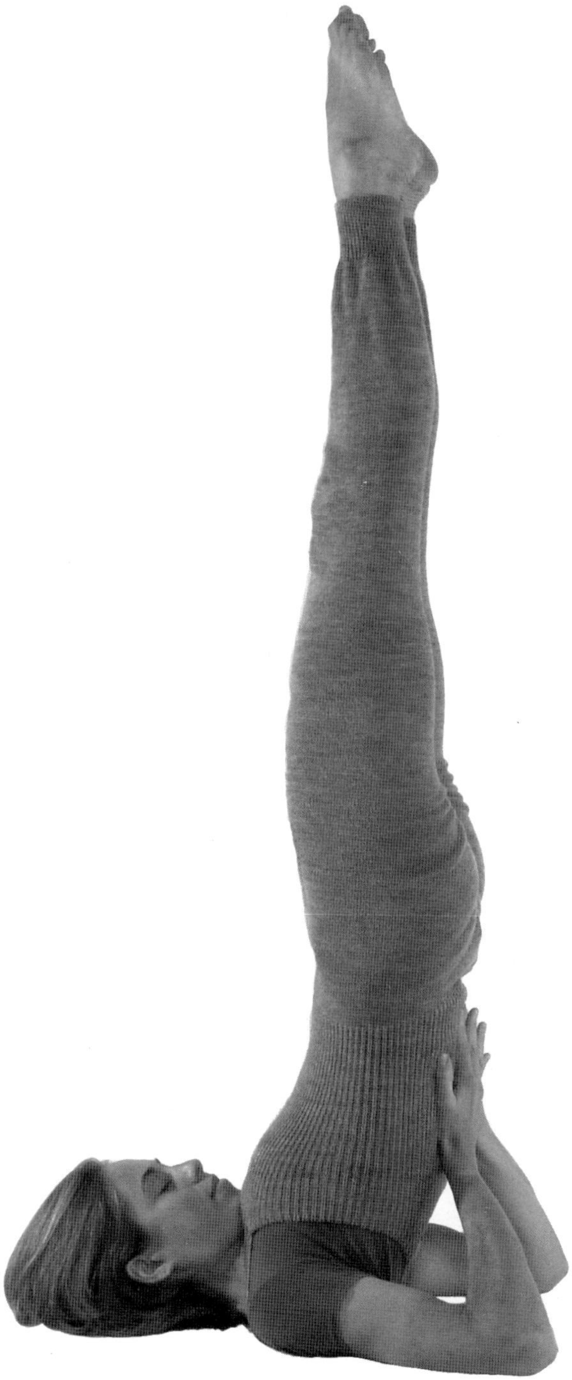

High shoulderstand
sarvanga asana

Starting pose

1 Lie on the back with the arms along the sides.

Into the pose

2 While breathing out, keep both legs extended and lift them and then the hips. When they are raised to a perpendicular position, straighten the body so that the back, hips and legs form a vertical line.

3 Support the back with the hands and drop the chin on to the chest.

4 Find the balance.

5 Keep knees straight and the ankles and toes extended during the entire pose.

Hold

6 In the beginning, hold the pose up to 15-30 seconds. Gradually increase to 60 seconds. Relax all muscles that are not required to keep the pose. Observe free and relaxed breathing.

Out

7 While breathing out, keep the legs straight and lower them towards the face. At the same time, place the hands on the ground, palms down.

8 While breathing in, slowly return to the starting pose by lowering the hips and letting the legs follow, keeping them straight.

9 Lie on the back to rest.

Headstand

sirs asana

Starting pose

1 Sit on the heels with the hands in the lap.

Into the pose

2 Link the hands and place the forearms on the ground in front of you so that the hands and the elbows form a triangle. Let the top of the forehead rest on the ground inside the triangle. Lift up the bottom.

3 Fit the crown of the head in against the palms and let the forehead rest on the ground.

4 Flex the ankles and place the toes on the ground. PICTURE 1

5 Lift the bottom higher and straighten the knees. PICTURE 2

6 Push the bottom over in the direction of the head, bend the knees and lift the feet off the ground when a balance point has been found. PICTURE 3

7 Place most of the body weight on the forearms and hands, with the forehead carrying a little less weight.

8 Stretch the legs upwards. Straighten the knees, ankles and toes.

PICTURE 1

PICTURE 2

Headstand

sirs asana

PICTURE 3

PICTURE 4

Hold

9 Do not stand in the pose more than 10-20 seconds to begin with. Later, the time may be increased up to 60 seconds. Observe free and relaxed breathing. PICTURE 4

Out

10 Bend the knees towards the stomach (PICTURE 3). From there, slowly stretch out the legs and let the feet touch the ground.

11 Place the fists on top of each other. Rest the forehead on the fists for about 30 seconds before raising the upper body.

The pose is best done on a relatively firm surface, such as a folded rug.

In the beginning, the headstand should be done against a wall to avoid falling over.

If the pose is not done correctly, it may strain the neck unduly. Ideally, the headstand should be learnt in a yoga class after the student has mastered a variety of other postures.

Photo: Ole Gjems-Onstad

BACKBENDS

Low cobra
bhujanga asana

Starting pose

1 Lie on the stomach with the forehead on the ground and the arms along the sides.

Into the pose

2 While breathing in, slowly lift the head, neck, shoulders and upper torso. Start with the head and neck, and let the arching movement pass slowly down the spine. Do not crane the head backwards.

3 When support becomes necessary, place the palms on the ground below the shoulders. Keep the elbows close to the sides. Use the back muscles to lift the upper body. The arms should not carry the weight; they should just give support and prevent the back from sinking.

4 Adjust the pose by letting the stomach rest on the ground so that the space between the shoulder blades remains arched.

Hold

5 Hold the pose for up to 30-60 seconds. Relax all muscles that are not required to maintain the pose. Observe free and relaxed breathing.

Out

6 While breathing out, place the arms by the sides and gradually lower the upper body until the forehead touches the ground. The movement should start at the base of the spine, then travel upwards to the shoulders, neck and eventually the head.

7 Rest while lying on the stomach with one cheek on the ground.

High cobra
bhujanga asana

Starting pose

1 Lie on the stomach with the forehead on the ground and the arms along the sides.

Into the pose

2 While breathing in, slowly lift the head, neck, shoulders and back. Start with the head and neck, and slowly let the arching movement pass down the spine. Place the hands below the shoulders to support the upper body. Use the back muscles to lift and hold the upper body as high as possible, and finally, push away with the hands to curve the entire spine.

Hold

3 Hold the pose for up to 30-60 seconds. Relax all muscles that are not needed to maintain the pose. Observe free and relaxed breathing.

Out

4 While breathing out, slowly and gradually lower the upper body. When the arms are no longer needed for support, place them along the sides. Let the downwards movement start at the base of the spine, passing upwards to the shoulders, neck and eventually the head. The final stage is when the forehead touches the ground.

5 Rest while lying on the stomach with one cheek on the ground.

Half bow
ardha dhanur asana

Starting pose

1 Lie on the stomach with the forehead on the ground and the arms along the sides.

Into the pose

2 Bend the right knee and grip the foot with the right hand.

3 Stretch the left arm out in front of the body. Keep the thighs together while doing the pose. PICTURE 1.

4 While breathing in, lift the head, upper body, right arm and leg to form a bow. Support the body with the left arm. Both sides of the pelvis should touch the ground.

Hold

5 Hold the pose for up to 30-60 seconds.

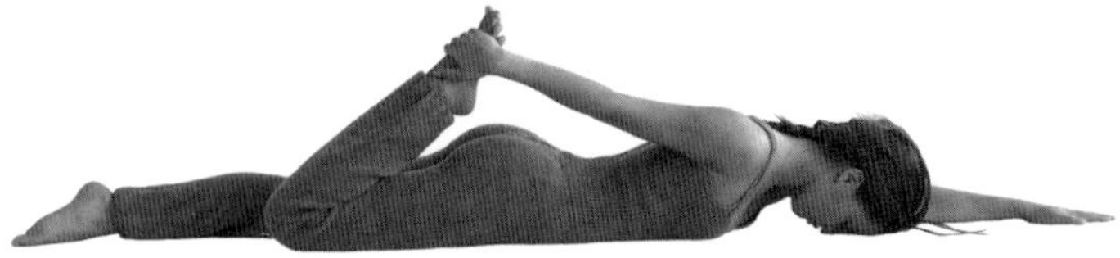

PICTURE 1

Relax all muscles that are not required to maintain the pose. Observe free and relaxed breathing. PICTURE 2

Out

6 While breathing out, gradually lower the body. Let go of the foot and extend the right leg. Place the arms by the sides and rest the forehead on the ground.

7 Repeat the pose on the opposite side by gripping the left foot.

8 Rest while lying on the stomach with one cheek on the ground.

PICTURE 2

Bow
dhanur asana

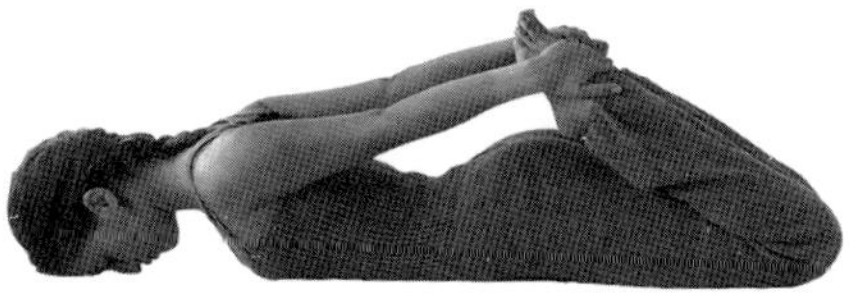

PICTURE 1

Starting pose

1 Lie on the stomach with the forehead on the ground and the arms along the sides.

Into the pose

2 Bend both knees and grip both feet or ankles with the hands. Keep the knees together while doing the pose. PICTURE 1

3 While breathing in, lift the head, arms and legs up from the ground so that the body forms a bow.

Hold

4 Hold the pose for up to 30-60 seconds. Relax all muscles that are not needed for the pose. Observe free and relaxed breathing. PICTURE 2

Out

5 While breathing out, slowly lower the body. Let go of the feet and stretch out the legs. Place the arms along the sides and rest the forehead on the ground.

6 Rest while lying on the stomach with one cheek on the ground.

PICTURE 2

Easier version:
Keep your knees apart.

Half camel

ardha ushtra asana

Starting pose

1 Sit on the heels with the hands in the lap.

Into the pose

2 Kneel upright. Keep the knees together while doing the entire pose.

3 Place the right hand on the right heel.

4 While breathing in, extend the left arm up and backwards, push the hips forward, lift the chest and curve the back.

Hold

5 Hold the pose for up to 30-60 seconds. Relax all muscles that are not needed to maintain the pose. Observe free and relaxed breathing.

Out

6 While breathing out, bring the left arm forwards and gradually return to the starting pose.

7 Repeat the pose by placing the left hand on the left heel and extending the right arm.

8 Rest while sitting on the heels with the hands in the lap.

Easier version:

Flex the ankles and place the toes on the ground. Do not bend the head backwards.

Camel
ushtra asana

Starting pose

1 Sit on the heels with the hands in the lap.

Into the pose

2 Kneel upright. Keep the knees together while doing the entire pose.

3 Place one hand on each heel.

4 While breathing in, push the hips forward and lift the chest until the body forms a bow.

Hold

5 Hold the pose for up to 30-60 seconds. Relax all muscles that are not needed to maintain the pose. Observe free and relaxed breathing.

Out

6 While breathing out, sit down on the heels and straighten the back.

7 Rest while sitting on the heels with the hands in the lap.

Easier version:
Flex the ankles and place the toes on the ground. Do not bend the head backwards.

Bridge

setu bandha asana

Starting pose

1 Lie on the back with the arms along the sides.

Into the pose

2 Bend the knees and place the soles of the feet close to the bottom. Keep the knees together while doing the pose.

3 While breathing in, lift the hips up.

4 Link the hands behind the back and stretch the arms towards the heels. Lift the chest up and tuck in the chin.

Hold

5 Hold the pose for up to 30-60 seconds. Relax all muscles that are not needed to maintain the pose. Observe free and relaxed breathing.

Out

6 Unlink the hands and place the arms by the sides.

7 While breathing out, slowly roll the back down. Start the movement at the top and lower the bottom last.

8 Extend the legs.

9 Lie on the back to rest.

Half fish

ardha matsya asana

Starting pose

1 Lie on the back with the arms along the sides.

Into the pose

2 Place the hands under the bottom with the palms down.

3 While breathing in, push away with the elbows and lift the chest up until the top of the head rests on the ground.

Hold

4 Hold the pose for up to 30-60 seconds. Relax all muscles that are not needed to maintain the pose. Observe free and relaxed breathing.

Out

5 While breathing out, slowly lower the back down to the ground.

6 Lie on the back to rest.

More challenging version:
Use "Sitting on the heels" (page 50) as the starting pose. Lean back on the elbows and curve the spine inwards (belly out) until the top of the head reaches the ground. Put the hands on the feet. Hold the pose before returning upwards to the starting pose.

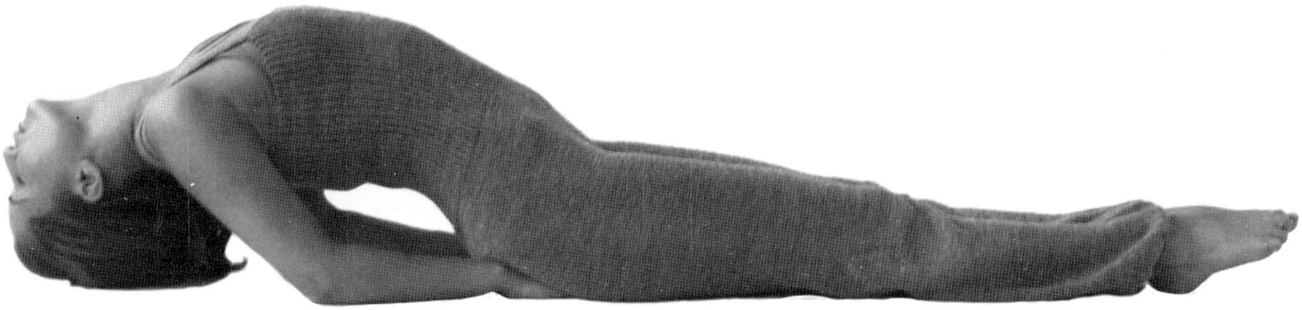

Half locust

ardha shalaba asana

Starting pose

1 Lie on the stomach with the forehead touching the ground and the arms along the sides. Keep the legs together.

Into the pose

2 While breathing in, stretch the right leg backwards and gradually lift it up. Let both sides of the pelvis rest on the ground. Place the arms along the sides or under the thighs with the palms facing up.

Hold

3 Hold the pose for up to 30-60 seconds. Relax all muscles that are not needed to maintain the pose. Hold the breath with the lungs half-filled with air. Observe the whole body.

Out

4 While gradually breathing out, slowly lower the leg.

5 Rest briefly. Do one cycle of full yoga breathing.

6 Repeat the posture using the left leg.

7 Rest while lying on the stomach with one cheek on the ground.

Locust

shalaba asana

Starting pose

1 Lie on the stomach with the forehead touching the ground and the arms along the sides. Keep the legs together.

Into the pose

2 When learning the pose, start by making fists and placing them under the hips. With more practice, place the arms along the sides. Always keep the knees together while doing this pose.

3 Breathe half-way in and hold the breath. Lift the legs up as far as possible whilst pushing hard with both hands so that the hips rise up from the ground. The forehead should rest firmly on the ground.

Hold

4 Hold the pose for up to 30-60 seconds. Relax all muscles that are not needed to maintain the pose. Observe the whole body.

Out

5 While breathing out, slowly lower the legs. Place the arms along the sides.

6 Rest while lying on the stomach with one cheek on the ground.

Half cobra
ardha bhujanga asana

Starting pose

1 Sit on the heels with the hands in the lap.

Into the pose

2 Lift bottom up and kneel upright.

3 Place the right foot well forward and keep a 90° angle in the right ankle.

4 Push the left leg backwards.

5 Lower the hips and straighten the upper body. Place both hands on the right knee.

Hold

6 Hold the pose for up to 30-60 seconds. Relax all muscles that are not needed to maintain the pose. Observe free and relaxed breathing.

Out

7 Bend the upper body forwards and place the hands on the ground on each side of the right foot.

8 Pull back the right knee and stand on the knees.

9 Repeat the pose with the left foot forward.

10 Rest while sitting on the heels with the hands in the lap.

Upward bow
urdhva dhanura asana

PICTURE 1

PICTURE 2

Starting pose

1 Lie on the back with the arms along the sides.

Into the pose

2 Bend the knees and place the feet on the ground.

3 Place the hands on the ground just behind the shoulders. **PICTURE 1**

4 While breathing deeply in, lift the stomach and chest until the body forms a high arch.

Hold

5 Hold the pose for up to 30-60 seconds. Relax all muscles that are not needed to maintain the pose. Observe free and relaxed breathing. **PICTURE 2**

Out

6 While breathing out, lower the body down to the ground.

7 Lie on the back to rest.

Photo: Karin Malmberg

FORWARD BENDS

Seated forward bend

paschimottana asana

Starting pose

1 Lie on the back with the arms along the sides.

Into the pose

2 Stretch both arms forward until they reach just above the knees. Lock thumbs.

3 While breathing in, gradually extend the arms above the head, then stretch them backwards until they reach the ground behind the head.

4 While breathing out, roll the back up from a lying to a sitting position. Keep the arms outstretched during this movement.

5 While breathing in, stretch the arms upwards. **PICTURE 1**

6 While breathing out, curve the body forward from the hips, keeping the back flat and the arms outstretched. Place the hands on the knees. **PICTURE 2**

7 Continue the movement whilst breathing out and arching the spine outward (belly in), so that the head moves towards the knees. Grip around the feet or calves.

Hold

8 Hold the pose for up to 30-60 seconds. Relax all muscles that are not needed to maintain the pose. Observe free and relaxed breathing. **PICTURE 3**

Out

9 Tuck the chin in towards the hollow of the throat.

10 While breathing in, let the palms slide up along the legs and roll the spine slowly up into a sitting position. Continue moving smoothly backwards until you are lying on the ground. Lift the chin from the chest last.

11 Lie on the back to rest.

PICTURE 1

PICTURE 2

PICTURE 3

Standing forward bend

padhasta asana

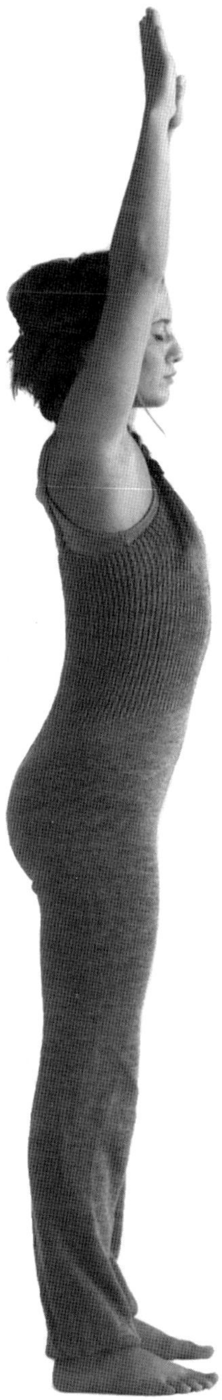

PICTURE 1

PICTURE 2

PICTURE 3

Starting pose

1 Stand with parallel legs and the arms hanging straight down at the sides.

Into the pose

2 Lock thumbs in front of you.

3 While breathing in, lift both arms and stretch them upwards. PICTURE 1

4 While breathing out, bend the upper body forwards from the hips, keeping the back straight as long as possible, and holding the head in a straight line with the back. PICTURE 2

5 Continue the movement by curving the spine and lowering the head towards the feet. Grip around the ankles or calves, and then tuck the upper body closer to the knees. With more practice, grip the toes.

Hold

6 Hold the pose for up to 30-60 seconds. Relax all muscles that are not needed to maintain the pose. Observe free and relaxed breathing. PICTURE 3

Out

7 Tuck the chin in towards the hollow of the throat.

8 While breathing in, slide the hands up the back of the legs and roll the spine slowly up into an upright position. Lift the chin last.

9 Return to the starting pose. Rest while standing with the feet together.

Seated sidebend (I)

janusir asana

Starting pose

1 Sit with outstretched legs.

Into the pose

2 Move the left foot towards the crotch and stretch the right leg to the side. Place the right hand on the left knee.

3 Straighten the back.

4 While breathing in, extend the left arm to the side and up.

5 While breathing out, lean the upper body and left arm towards the right leg.

6 Twist the back so that the chest and face turn slightly upwards.

Hold

7 Hold the pose for up to 30-60 seconds. Relax all muscles that are not needed to maintain the pose. Observe free and relaxed breathing.

Out

8 While breathing in, stretch the left arm slowly upwards and straighten the upper body. Lower the arm while breathing out.

9 Return to the starting pose.

10 Rest for a short while. Do one cycle of full yoga breathing.

11 Repeat the posture on the opposite side.

12 Lie on the back to rest.

Seated sidebend (II)

janusir asana

Starting pose

1 Sit with outstretched legs.

Into the pose

2 Move the left foot towards the crotch and stretch the right leg out to the side.

3 Straighten the back and twist the upper body towards the right.

4 Lock thumbs.

5 While breathing in, extend the arms upwards.

6 While breathing out, lean the upper body slowly forwards towards the right leg as far as possible. Keep the back straight. Lower the arms to the right leg.

7 Hold the pose with the back straight for a short while. Observe free and relaxed breathing.

8 While breathing out, bend the back and head towards the right knee. Grip around the foot or calf.

Hold

9 Hold the pose for up to 30-60 seconds. Relax all muscles that are not needed to maintain the pose. Observe free and relaxed breathing.

Out

10 Tuck the chin in towards the hollow of the throat.

11 While breathing in, release the foot and let the hands slide up along the sides of the right leg while rolling the spine upwards.

12 Rest for a short while. Do one cycle of full yoga breathing.

13 Repeat the posture on the opposite side.

14 Lie on the back to rest.

Plough

hala asana

Starting pose

1 Lie on the back with the arms along the sides.

Into the pose

2 While breathing out, slowly lift both outstretched legs up over the head and backwards until the feet touch the ground.

3 Place the palms on the back for support.

Hold

4 Hold the pose for up to 30-60 seconds. Keep the legs extended. Relax all muscles that are not needed to maintain the pose. Observe free and relaxed breathing.

Out

5 Place the palms on the ground.

6 While breathing in, slowly roll the spine back down and lower the hips into the starting pose. Let the outstretched legs pass as close to the face as possible.

7 Lie on the back to rest.

Easier version:
Bend the knees slightly while lifting or lowering the legs.

Dog

adho mukha svana asana

Starting pose

1 Sit on the heels with the hands in the lap.

Into the pose

2 Kneel up on all fours with flexed ankles and with the toes on the ground.

3 Lift the bottom up into the air, keeping the legs and arms outstretched and the palms on the ground, so that the body forms a triangle.

4 Lower the heels towards the ground and draw the chest closer to the knees.

Hold

5 Hold the pose for up to 30-60 seconds. Relax all muscles that are not needed to maintain the pose. Observe free and relaxed breathing.

Out

6 Bend the knees and lower the back so as to return to the starting pose.

7 Rest while sitting on the heels with the hands in the lap.

The posture is also a part of the sun salutation (page 96).

Photo: Ole Gjems-Onstad

TWIST POSTURES

Twist (I)

vakra asana

Starting pose

1 Sit with outstretched legs.

Into the pose

2 Bend the right knee, take the right leg over the left leg and place the sole of the right foot outside the left knee.

3 Hook the left elbow around the right knee. Straighten the back.

4 While breathing in, lift the outstretched right arm forwards and up to eye level.

5 While breathing out, look over the right shoulder and twist the spine so as to take the right arm as far as possible behind you. Then lower the arm and place the hand on the ground just behind the bottom. Let the attention follow the movement of the hand. Make sure that the entire spine is twisted and that it is relatively straight.

Hold

6 Hold the pose for up to 30-60 seconds. Relax all muscles that are not needed to maintain the pose. Observe free and relaxed breathing.

Out

7 While breathing in, slowly lift the right arm up to eye level, with the hand pointing backwards.

8 While breathing out, slowly untwist the spine and turn round to the front again. At the end of this movement, lower the arm. Let the attention follow the movement of the hand in a restful manner throughout this process.

9 Uncross the legs, stretch out the right leg and rest for a few seconds.

10 Repeat the posture on the opposite side.

11 Lie on the back to rest.

Twist (II)
ardha matsyendra asana

Starting pose

1 Sit with outstretched legs.

Into the pose

2 Bring the left foot towards the crotch.

3 Take the right leg over the left leg and place the sole of the right foot outside the left knee.

4 Place the left elbow on the outside of the right knee and grip around the ankle. Straighten the back.

5 While breathing in, extend the right arm and lift it to eye level. PICTURE 1

6 While breathing out, look over the right shoulder and twist the spine to the right so as to take the right arm as far as possible behind you (PICTURE 2). Then lower the arm and place the hand on the ground just behind the bottom. Let the attention follow the movement of the hand. Make sure that the spine is twisted and kept relatively straight.

Hold

7 Hold the pose for up to 30-60 seconds. Relax all muscles that are not needed to maintain the pose. See if the twist can be increased slightly without too much effort. Observe free and relaxed breathing. PICTURE 3

Out

8 While breathing in, slowly lift the right arm up to eye level. Let the hand point directly backwards.

9 While breathing out, gradually untwist the spine and turn slowly round to the front again. At the end of this movement, lower the arm and place the right hand on top of the left. Let the attention follow the movement of the hand throughout this process.

10 Stretch the legs and rest for a little while.

11 Repeat the posture on the opposite side.

12 Lie on the back to rest.

PICTURE 1

PICTURE 2

PICTURE 3

Reclining twist (I)

Starting pose

1 Lie on the back with the arms along the sides.

Into the pose

2 Extend the arms to each side of the body at shoulder level, palms down.

3 Bend the knees up, keeping the feet together on the ground.

4 While breathing out, lower the knees to the right until they touch the ground while turning the head in the opposite direction, i.e. to the left side.

5 While breathing in, gradually raise the knees to a central position.

6 While breathing out, lower the knees to the left side and turn the head to the right.

7 Slowly repeat these movements several times on each side while breathing calmly and regularly.

Out

8 Extend the legs until they are flat on the ground.

9 Lie on the back to rest.

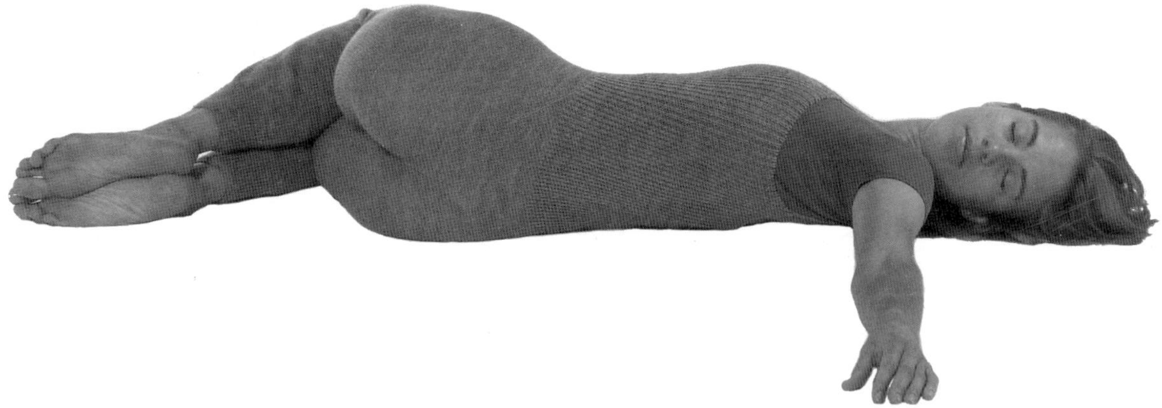

Reclining twist (II)

Starting pose

1 Lie on the back with the arms along the sides.

Into the pose

2 Extend the arms to each side of the body at shoulder level, palms down.

3 Raise the legs so as to make 90° angles at the knees and hips.

4 While breathing out, lower the bent legs to the ground on the right side while turning the head to the left.

5 While breathing in, raise the bent legs to a central position.

6 While breathing out, lower the bent legs all the way to the left and turn the head to the right.

7 Slowly repeat several times on each side while breathing calmly and regularly.

Out

8 Extend the legs until they are flat on the ground.

9 Lie on the back to rest.

Triangle

trikona asana

Starting pose

1 Stand with the legs together and the arms along the sides.

Into the pose

2 Move the right foot aside so that the legs are slightly more than hip width apart.

3 While breathing in, lift the arms to shoulder level at the sides. **PICTURE 1**

4 While breathing out, bend the upper body forwards until it forms a 90° angle to the legs. Keep the back straight and the arms out to the sides.

5 Breathe in.

6 While breathing out, rotate the upper body so that the right arm touches the left foot or leg and the left arm points upwards. Look up towards the left hand. Keep a 90° angle between the legs and upper body throughout this process.

Hold

7 Hold the pose for up to 30-60 seconds. Relax all muscles that are not needed to maintain the pose. Observe free and relaxed breathing. **PICTURE 2**

Out

8 While breathing in, turn the upper body back to the middle position, still bending forward with the arms straight out to the sides.

9 While breathing out, rotate to the right so as to repeat the posture on the other side.

10 Stop in the central position.

11 While breathing out, lower both arms and slowly roll up the spine with the chin against the chest.

12 Stand in the starting pose to rest.

PICTURE 2

Triangle
trikona asana

PICTURE 1

Photo: Karin Malmberg

BALANCE POSTURES

Tree (I)

vriksha asana

Starting pose

1 Stand with the legs together and the arms along the sides.

Into the pose

2 Let the gaze rest effortlessly on a point in front of you.

3 Place the right foot on top of the left foot. PICTURE 1

4 Pull the right foot slowly up the inside of the left leg and find your balance (PICTURE 2). The foot may be pulled all the way up to the thigh. Keep the sole of the foot resting against the thigh and let the knee point to the side.

5 While breathing in, lift the outstretched arms to the sides. Then raise the arms above the head and place the palms together.

Hold

6 Adjust the balance and hold the pose for up to 30-60 seconds. Relax all muscles that are not needed to maintain the pose. Observe free and relaxed breathing (PICTURE 3). With practice, try to stand with closed eyes.

Out

7 While breathing out, extend and lower the arms.

8 Let the right leg slide slowly down the inside of the left leg until the foot touches the ground.

9 Repeat the posture on the opposite side.

10 Stand in the starting pose to rest.

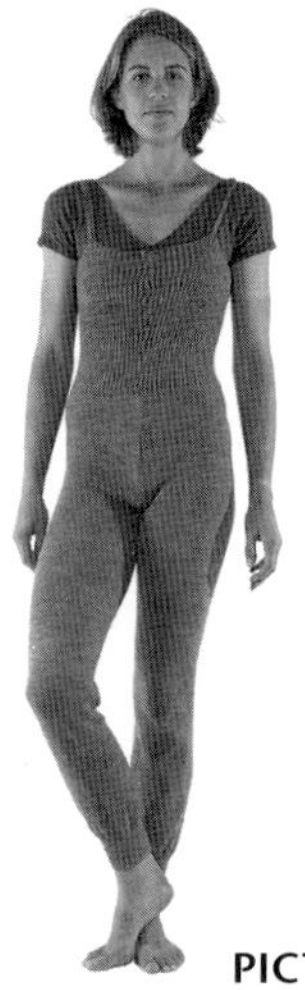

PICTURE 1

PICTURE 2

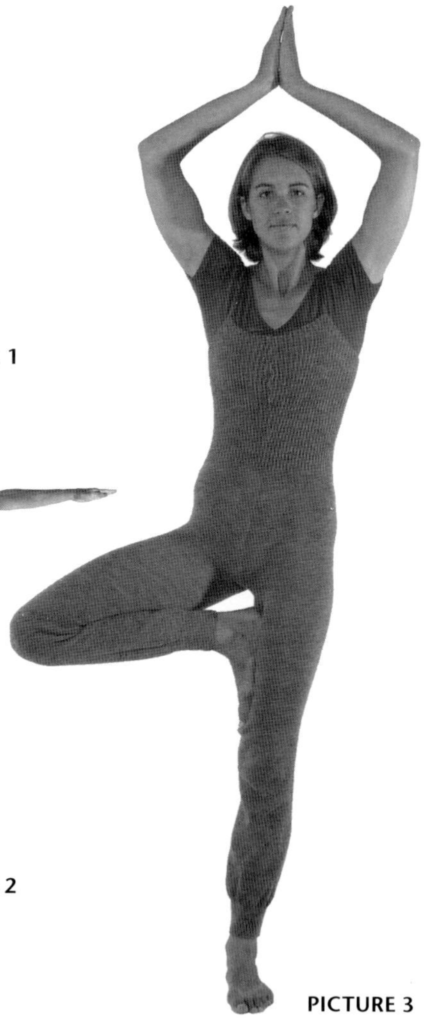

PICTURE 3

Tree (II)
vriksha asana

PICTURE 1

PICTURE 2

Starting pose

1 Stand with the legs together and the arms at the sides.

Into the pose

2 Let the gaze rest effortlessly on a point in front of you.

3 Transfer the body weight on to the left leg.

4 Bend the right leg up behind and grip around the foot or ankle with the right hand. Do not let the foot move to the side.

5 While breathing in, lift the left arm and extend it straight out in front of you. **PICTURE 1**

6 While breathing out, curve the upper body by leaning forwards and lift the right arm and leg until the upper body and leg form a bow. Continue to stretch the left arm forwards.

Hold

7 Adjust the balance and rest in the pose for 10-60 seconds. Relax all muscles that are not needed to maintain the pose. Observe free and relaxed breathing. With practice, try to do the pose with closed eyes. **PICTURE 2**

Out

8 While breathing out, gradually return to the starting pose. Finally, release the foot.

9 Repeat the posture on the opposite side.

10 Stand in the starting pose to rest.

Photo: Ole Gjems-Onstad

COMBINED POSTURES

Thunder pose

1 Sit on the heels with the hands in the lap. **PICTURE 1**

2 Link the hands behind the back and extend the arms. **PICTURE 2**

3 While breathing in, lift the chest and curve the spine backwards.

4 While breathing out, slowly bend the upper body forwards, keeping the spine curved. Continue until the forehead rests on the ground. Stretch the arms backwards and up. **PICTURE 3**

5 Hold the pose for a short while. Breathe freely.

6 While breathing in, tuck the chin against the hollow of the throat. Roll the spine gradually up again. **PICTURE 4**

7 When the body has reached the vertical position, breathe out and continue the movement by leaning slightly backwards. Put the fingers or palms on the ground behind the feet for support.

8 While breathing in, lift the chest slightly and pull the shoulder blades together. Tuck the chin towards the hollow of the throat or carefully tilt the head backwards. **PICTURE 5**

9 While breathing out, move the upper body forwards until the forehead rests on the ground. At the same time, stretch the arms forwards. **PICTURE 6**

10 Hold the pose for a short while. Breathe freely.

11 While breathing in, tuck the chin against the hollow of the throat. Gradually roll up the spine to return to the starting pose.

12 Place the hands in the lap and rest. **PICTURE 7**

Move in a slow, flowing manner, accompanied by deep breath and preferably with your eyes closed.

PICTURE 1

PICTURE 5

Thunder pose

PICTURE 2

PICTURE 3

PICTURE 4

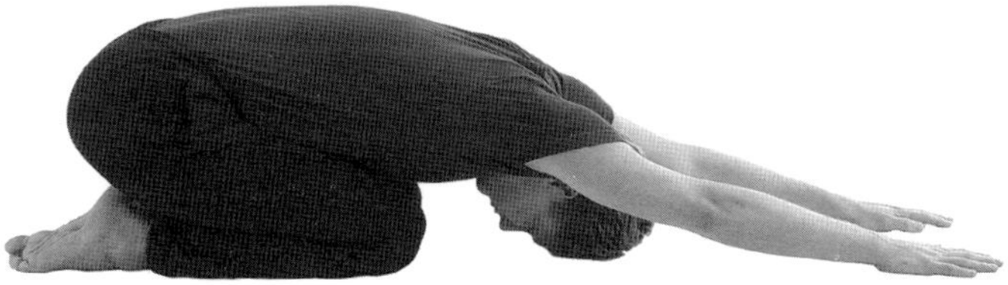

PICTURE 6

PICTURE 7

Sun salutation

surya namaskar

1 Stand with the legs together. Place the palms together in front of the chest, fingers pointing up. **PICTURE 1**

2 While breathing out, lower the arms in front of the body. Lock thumbs.

3 While breathing in, lift the arms and stretch them above the head. Arch the body backwards. **PICTURE 2**

4 While breathing out, bend forwards until the hands touch the feet or ankles, and the head touches the knees (if possible). **PICTURE 3**

5 While breathing in, take a long step backwards with the right foot. Curve the head and the upper body as in the cobra pose. **PICTURE 4**

6 While breathing out, move the left foot backwards and place it next to the right foot. Lift the hips so that the bottom points upwards. Pull the head and chest towards the knees. Lower the heels to the ground. **PICTURE 5**

7 With empty lungs, hold the breath for several seconds. Bend the elbows and lower the body until the knees, chest and forehead touch the ground. The bottom remains slightly lifted. **PICTURE 6**

8 While breathing in, straighten the arms and press away from the ground so as to lift the chest and shoulders. Curve the head and upper body backwards as in the high cobra pose. **PICTURE 7**

9 While breathing out, lift the hips to the same pose as in point 6. **PICTURE 8**

10 While breathing in, step forwards with the right leg so that the foot is between the hands. Lower the hips towards the ground, keeping a slight curve in the back. Lift the head and upper body as in the cobra pose. **PICTURE 9**

11 While breathing out, bring the left foot forwards to join the right foot. Drop the head to the knees (if possible). **PICTURE 10**

12 While breathing in, roll the body upwards with the chin against the hollow of the throat. Let the hands slide along the legs. Stretch the arms above the head and arch the upper body backwards. **PICTURE 11**

13 While breathing out, put the palms together in front of the chest, fingers up. **PICTURE 12**

14 Repeat the postures by starting with the opposite leg.

When one round is finished, go directly on to the next, but start with the opposite leg. Breathe deeply in and out throughout the sequence except for the short time when the breath is held. The breathing should be strong and coordinated with the movements.

When all parts have been mastered, this exercise may be done faster and repeated several times. Lie down and rest for 2-3 minutes on the back after every 10 rounds or so.

Sun salutation
surya namaskar

PICTURE 1

PICTURE 2

PICTURE 3

PICTURE 4

PICTURE 5

PICTURE 6

PICTURE 7

PICTURE 8

PICTURE 9

PICTURE 10

PICTURE 11

PICTURE 12

Photo: Karin Malmberg

OTHER POSTURES

Dorsal hand hold

Starting pose

1 Sit with the legs crossed or sit on the heels.

Into the pose

2 Place the left hand on the lower back, palm out, and slide it as far up the back as possible.

3 While breathing in, raise the right arm straight up. While breathing out, bend the elbow and lower the hand behind the neck.

4 Try to get the hands to meet behind the back. Lock fingers if possible.

Hold

5 Rest in the pose while doing 3 full cycles of yoga breathing.

Out

6 Release the hand grip.

7 While breathing in, lift the right arm straight up. Move the left arm back to the front of the body.

8 While breathing out, slowly lower the arms and place them in the lap.

9 Sit and rest for a few seconds.

10 Repeat the posture using the opposite arm.

11 Place the hands in the lap and rest.

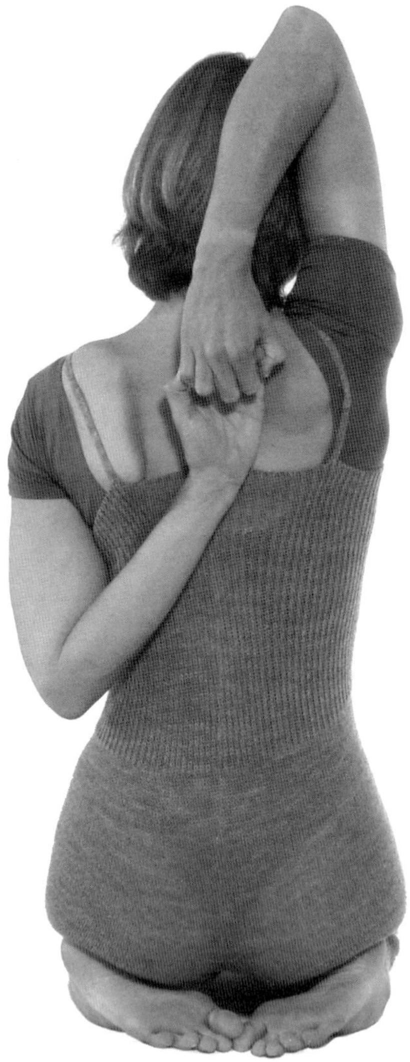

Shoulder roll

1. Sit with the legs crossed or sit on the heels.
2. Place one hand on each shoulder, on the fingertips, and relax. **PICTURE 1.**
3. Make large circles with the elbows.
4. Bring the elbows forwards to touch each other in front of the chest. **PICTURE 2**
5. While breathing calmly in, separate the elbows and lift them above shoulder height. **PICTURE 3**
6. While breathing out, move the elbows backwards and then down.
7. Repeat the circles slowly in the same direction 5 times.
8. Reverse direction and repeat 5 times.
9. Place the hands in the lap and rest.

PICTURE 1

PICTURE 2

PICTURE 3

Head roll

1 Sit with the legs crossed, on the heels, or in a chair.
2 Look straight forwards and close the eyes. **PICTURE 1**
3 While breathing out, bend the head forwards. **PICTURE 2**
4 While breathing in, roll the head towards the right shoulder and turn the face up slightly. **PICTURE 3**
5 While breathing out, roll the head back down to the middle. **PICTURE 2**
6 While breathing in again, roll the head slightly upwards to the left.
7 Repeat 5 times, changing direction each time.
8 Lift up the head and rest in the starting pose.
9 The rolling should be done slowly and carefully without force and from side to side. Make sure that the head is not bent backwards.

PICTURE 1

PICTURE 2

PICTURE 3

Eye practices
brumadhya drishti

Sit with your legs crossed or sit in a chair, with your hands in your lap. Repeat the movements 3-7 times at a relaxed but even pace. After you have completed one practice, close your eyes and then rest, with your fingers very lightly pressing your eyelids.

Practice I – side movements

1 Look straight in front with a soft, restful gaze.

2 While breathing in, calmly move the eyes as far as possible to the right.

3 While breathing out, move slowly back to the central position and look straight in front.

4 While breathing in, move the eyes calmly as far as possible to the left.

5 While breathing out, move back to the central position.

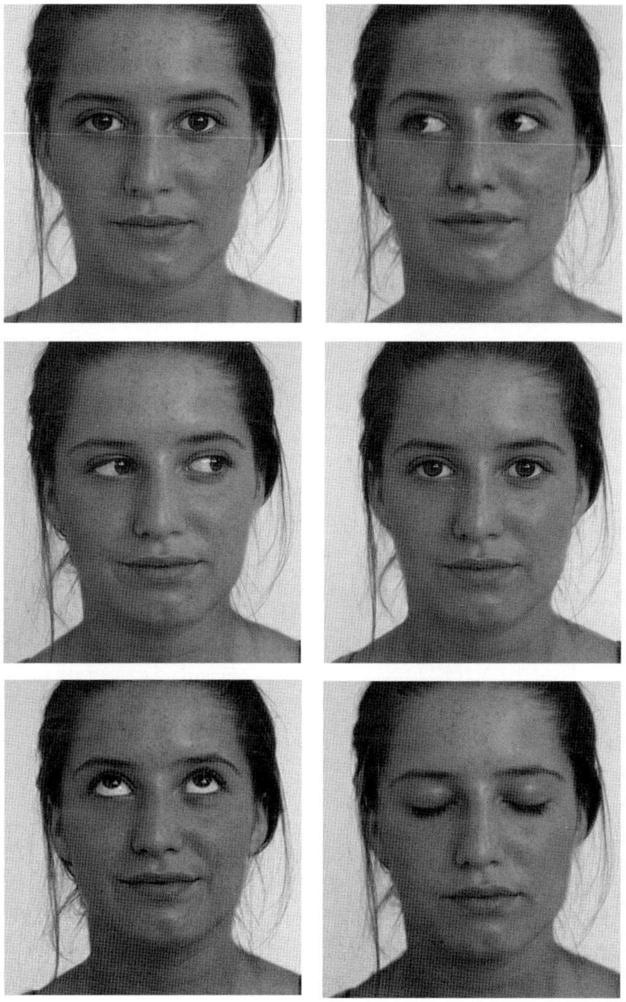

Practice II – vertical movements

Start in the same way. Look up as far as possible towards the eyebrows while breathing in, then down as far as possible towards the chest while breathing out.

Practice III – rolling movements

Let the eyes make large circular movements, first to the right, then up, then to the left, then down and back to the starting point. Breathe in when lifting the gaze, and out when lowering it.

Change the direction for each repetition.

Abdominal lock

uddiyana bhanda

Starting pose

1 Stand with the legs together and the arms along the sides.

Into the pose

2 Place the feet a little more than hip width apart and bend the knees slightly.

3 Curve the upper body forwards and put the hands on the knees.

4 Draw the breath in, as in the first part of the yoga breathing cycle.

5 Empty the lungs as fully as possible by exhaling forcefully. When the lungs feel empty, hold the breath whilst firmly pulling in the stomach so that the diaphragm is lifted.

Hold

6 Hold the breath with the stomach retracted for 10-30 seconds.

Out

7 Breathe in, let the stomach out, and return to the upright position.

8 Do full yoga breathing three times before, if you wish, repeating this bhanda or abdominal contraction.

9 Lie on the back to rest.

Stomach waves

Starting pose

1 Lie on the back with the arms along the sides.

Into the pose

2 Bend and raise the knees with the feet on the ground and the legs slightly apart.

3 Exhale completely, then firmly pull in the stomach. PICTURE 1

Hold

4 Hold the breath while moving the stomach in and out several times as quickly as possible. Keep going for 20-30 seconds. PICTURES 2 AND 1

Out

5 Breathe in. Do two cycles of full yoga breathing before repeating.

6 Lie on the back to rest.

PICTURE 2

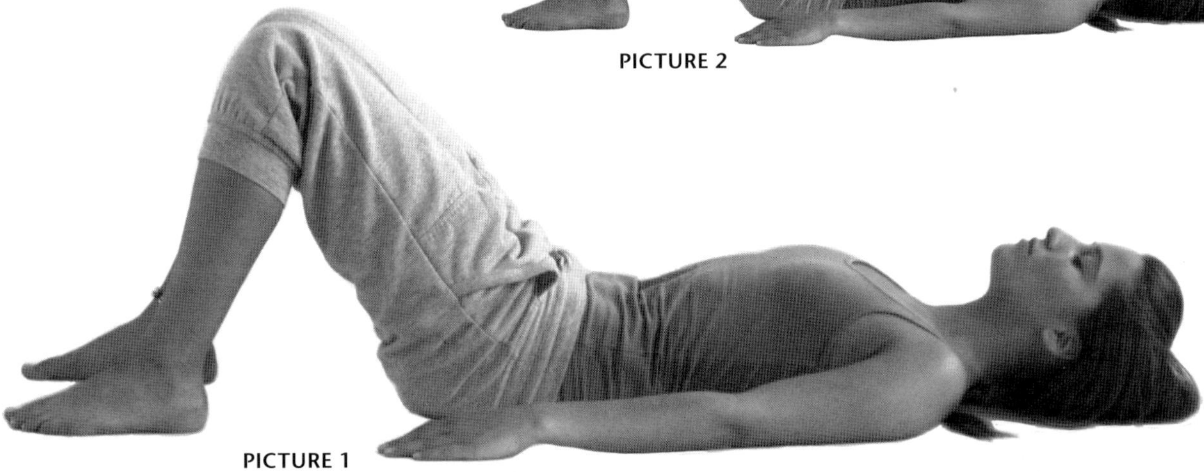

PICTURE 1

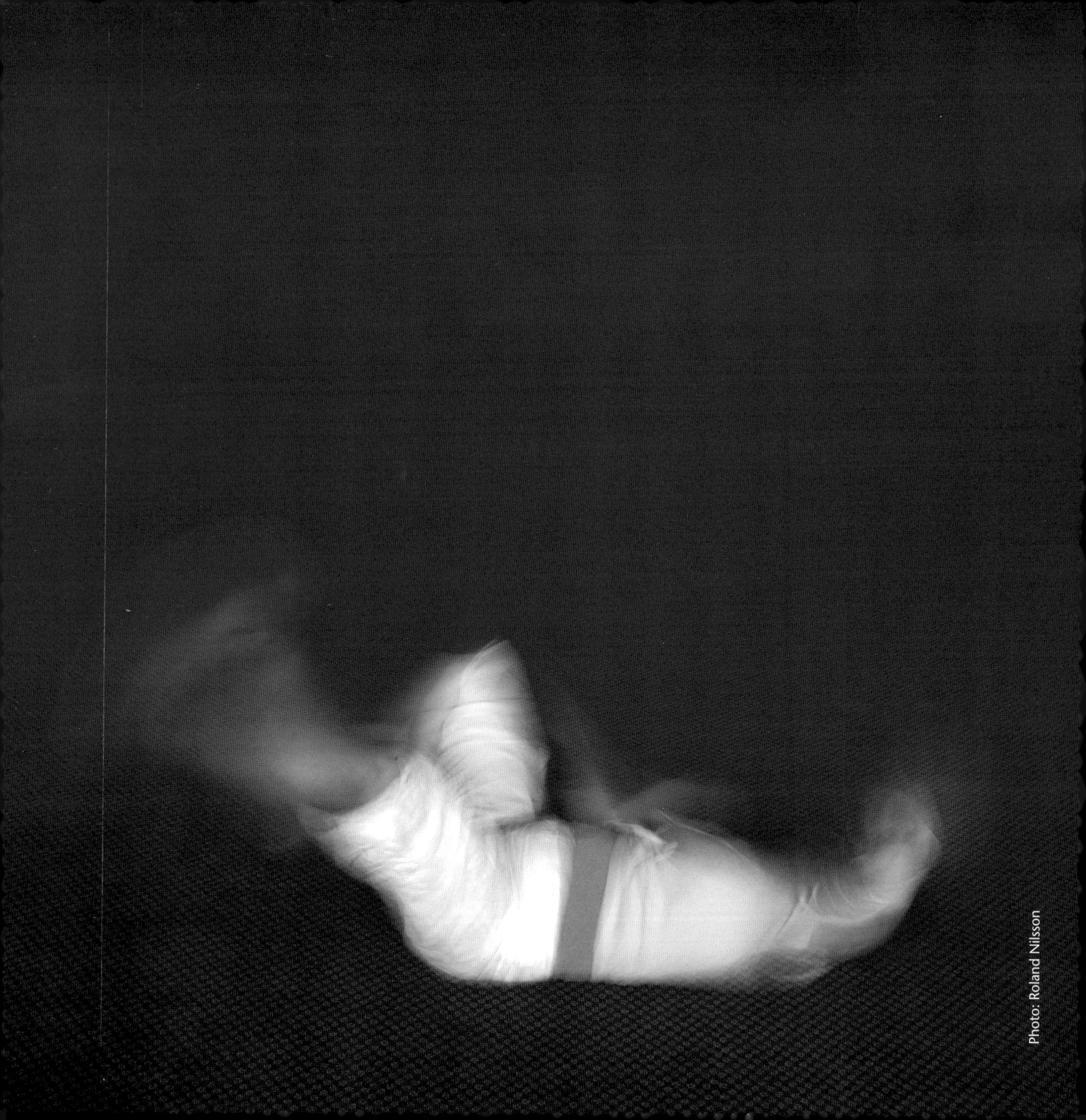

Photo: Roland Nilsson

IMPULSE PRACTICES

Impulsive slow twist (I)

1 Lie on the back with the arms along the sides.
2 Let the attention travel to the face. Become aware of the subtle sensations, impulses, tiredness and tensions that may be there.
3 Let those sensations or impulses be expressed in slow movements or grimaces. Allow the facial muscles to twitch, contract and stretch freely.
4 Gradually involve the fingers, toes, hands, arms and feet as extensions of the facial movements.
5 Continue extending the movements to more body parts until the entire body is involved. Breathe freely.
6 Continue for 1-3 minutes.
7 Lie on the back to rest.

Impulsive slow twist (II)

1 Lie on the back with the arms along the sides.
2 Let the attention travel to the abdomen. Become aware of the sensations, impulses or tensions that may be there.
3 Release these sensations or impulses from the abdomen and give them expression in slow movements out towards the rest of the body.
4 Gradually involve the chest and hips, arms and legs.
5 Eventually, let the entire body participate. Breathe freely.
6 Continue for 1-3 minutes.
7 Lie on the back to rest.

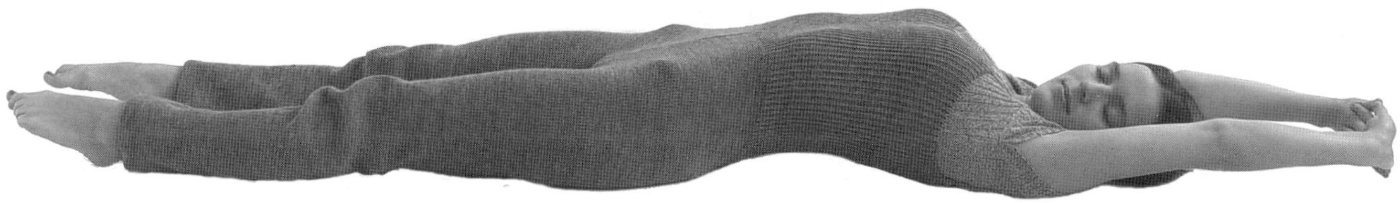

Rapid shaking

1. Lie on the back with the arms along the sides.
2. Lift the arms and legs.
3. Let the attention rest on your feelings at this moment. Notice emotions, moods and frustrations.
4. Release these feelings to be expressed as shaking movements of the arms and legs. Gradually increase the speed and intensity until the arms and legs are shaking as fast as possible. Finally, allow the breathing to be impulsive too; breathe fast and intensively. Let the whole body participate in these rapid movements.
5. Continue for 1-3 minutes.
6. Stop all rapid movements, and lower the arms and legs.
7. Lie on the back to rest.

Impulse practice may be done in several ways. Any part of the body can be chosen as the starting point, e.g., the legs, hands, tongue, hips. Letting these body parts loose and shaking them is the first stage.

The next stage is giving the entire body a chance to participate in the shaking movements.

The final and most challenging stage is to let loose the impulses in the breathing as well as the body movements. This may lead to hyperventilation and discomfort, in which case stop, breathe slowly and hold the breath for 10-20 heartbeats between each breath until the discomfort subsides.

Rapid shaking

Photo: Roland Nilsson

RESTING POSTURES

Corpse
sava asana

1 Lie comfortably on the back with the legs extended and the arms along the sides.

2 Turn the palms up and make sure that the entire body is relaxing whilst resting firmly on the ground.

3 Keep the eyes closed and let the mind with its thoughts, feelings, sensations and images wander freely. Do this for 5-10 minutes.

At the end of any sequence of yoga postures (or programme), the student should lie down in the corpse pose.

With a free mental attitude, the body and mind are given the opportunity to go into a spontaneous meditation instigated by the yoga sequence. The meditative deepening in this resting pose is not achieved by controlling thoughts or breathing. There is no use of images, mantras or meditation sounds. The meditative momentum results from the sequence of yoga postures. Provided the mind is given unrestricted freedom to drift wherever it wants, meditation occurs spontaneously.

The corpse pose should be done on a relatively firm surface, for example a yoga mat or rug. The effect will not be the same if lying on a soft mattress.

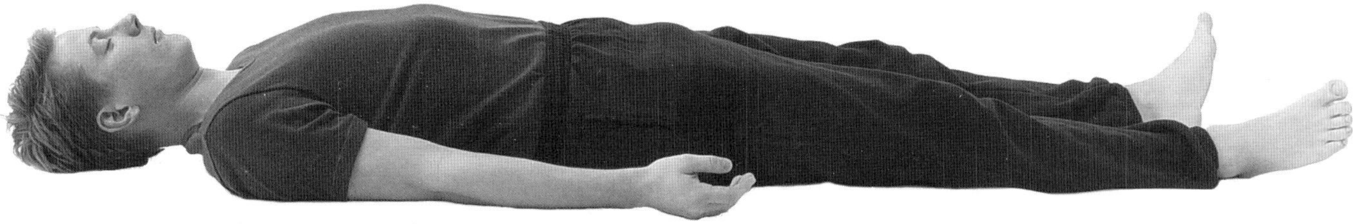

Sideways rest and Prone rest

Sideways rest

1 Lie on the right side of the body with the left arm under the head, while bending up the left knee.

2 Let the right arm rest with the palm facing up.

This restorative pose can be used for rest during any yoga programme.

Prone rest

1 Lie on the stomach with one cheek on the ground.

2 Place the arms along the sides, and let the heels fall slightly apart.

This restorative pose follows naturally after postures carried out whilst lying on the stomach.

Photo: Roland Nilsson

SITTING POSTURES

Sitting cross legged and on the heels

Sitting cross legged

SUKHA ASANA

1 Sit with crossed legs. The left leg should be on the inside.
2 Keep the lower back straight.
3 Let the knees come down towards the ground and make sure that the hips are relaxed.
4 Let the hands rest in the lap with the palms up.
5 Observe the breath.

The pose becomes easier and more comfortable if the bottom is lifted slightly by means of a cushion, a blanket or similar. Alternatively, comfort may be enhanced by placing a small cushion or a blanket between the knees and feet.

This is an excellent posture for meditation, attention training and several breathing practices. If meditating in this pose, the lower back should be given enough support to free the student from paying attention to the way he is sitting. This is also a starting pose (page 50).

Sitting on the heels

VARJA ASANA

1 Kneel upright.
2 Keep the knees and thighs together.
3 Cross the big toes and turn the heels out slightly.
4 Sit down on the heels and find the balance.
5 Let the hands rest in the lap, palms up.
6 Observe the breath.

This is a good posture for attention training and breathing practice. It is also a starting pose (page 50).

Half and full lotus

Half lotus

ARDHA PADMA ASANA

1 Sit with the legs extended.
2 Bring the left foot in towards the crotch.
3 Bend the right knee. Grip the right ankle and lift the leg slightly before placing the foot on top of the left leg, letting the heel touch the abdomen.
4 Let the knees drop towards the ground. Keep the hips relaxed.
5 Let the hands rest in the lap with the palms up.
6 Observe the breath.
7 The pose will be easier and more comfortable if the bottom is slightly lifted by means of a blanket, cushion or similar.

This is a good pose for attention training and breathing practice.

Lotus

PADMA ASANA

No beginner should try to get into the full lotus pose without proper instructions. This posture is primarily for advanced students of yoga who are quite fit and have developed a supple body. It involves a major strain on the knees and may be harmful. Any effort to master this pose must progress slowly and unhurriedly.

Photo: Karin Malmberg

BREATHING PRACTICES

Yoga breathing

The cycle of yoga breathing has three parts, each of which should be learned separately before they are joined together. Ideally, the student should practise daily until the transitions between the three parts can be made smoothly and effortlessly.

Breathing should be done through the nose, providing it is not congested. When practising, relax the jaws, tongue and throat. Closing or half-closing the eyes gives a stronger inward focus. Yoga breathing should be done without strain, and while lying down, sitting or standing. To begin with, it is advisable to lie on the back. Placing the hands on the abdomen or ribs is helpful initially; it will make the novice become aware of how to move with ease through the three parts.

At the outset, a sequence of yoga postures should start with seven cycles of full yoga breathing. During this time, all the blood in the body is likely to have passed at least once through the lungs. In addition, yoga breathing should be done 2-3 times after the short rest between the postures in any yoga sequence.

Part 1: Abdominal breathing

1 Lie on the back. Initially, place the palms on each side of the abdomen close to the navel in order to register the breathing movements. **PICTURE 1**

2 Breathe calmly and regularly so that the abdomen expands. The chest should not participate in inhalation in part 1.

3 When breathing out, release the breath naturally and effortlessly.

4 Rest for a few seconds before starting the next breath.

5 Repeat 5-10 times.

The movements of the abdomen are caused by contractions in the ring-shaped muscles of the two domes of the diaphragm. With these movements, the organs in the abdomen are pushed gently down and out while the lungs are filled with air.

Part 2: Costal breathing

1 Lie on the back. Initially, place one palm on each set of ribs in order to register their movements when breathing. PICTURE 2
2 Breathe in calmly and regularly so that the chest expands. Make sure that the breathing only involves the ribs. This can be checked by pushing the hands firmly against the ribs.
3 When breathing out, release the breath naturally and effortlessly.
4 Rest for a few seconds before starting the next breath.
5 Repeat 5-10 times.

PICTURE 1

PICTURE 2

Part 3: High costal breathing

1 Lie on the back. Initially, place the palms on the upper chest to register the breathing movements. PICTURE 3
2 Breathe in calmly and regularly so that the upper part of the chest expands a little and subsequently the shoulders are lifted.
3 When breathing out, release the breath naturally and effortlessly.
4 Rest for a few seconds before starting the next breath.
5 Repeat 5-10 times.

PICTURE 3

Full yoga breathing

In full yoga breathing, the three parts of yoga breathing (pages 122-123) are combined into one continuous, gliding movement. Each part should flow smoothly into the next, starting in the abdomen and travelling upwards via the ribs to the shoulders. The lungs will then be filled with air.

1 Lie on the back with the arms along the sides.
2 Start breathing in so that the abdomen expands (abdominal breathing, page 122).
3 Continue breathing in so that the chest expands (costal breathing, page 123).
4 From the ribs, continue upwards, breathing in slowly through the upper body, involving the shoulders and collar bones (high costal breathing, page 123).
5 Rest for a brief moment with full lungs before relaxing and exhaling passively, letting the breath flow out calmly and continuously.
6 Repeat 7 times.
7 Rest while lying on the back.

When learning full yoga breathing, follow the movements of the breath upwards through the body by placing the hands first on the abdomen, then on the ribs and finally on the upper part of the chest. Once the breathing can be performed with ease, it may be done in a sitting position, for example with the legs crossed, on the heels or in the half lotus pose.

Full yoga breathing

Joyful breathing

sukha purvak

Joyful breathing (I)

1 Sit cross-legged, on the heels or in the half lotus.
2 Apply light pressure to the outside of the right nostril using the right thumb.
3 Calmly breathe out through the left nostril, and then in again.
4 Transfer the pressure to the left nostril using the middle and ring fingers, removing the thumb from the nose.
5 Calmly breathe out and then in again through the right nostril.
6 Breathe effortlessly through alternate nostrils for a few minutes.

Joyful breathing (II)

1 Sit cross-legged, on the heels or in the half lotus.

Left nostril

2 Apply light pressure to the outside of the right nostril using the right thumb. Place the index finger on the forehead a little above the eyebrows in the midline between the eyes.
3 Breathe out calmly through the left nostril, counting 8 heartbeats.
4 Hold the breath, counting 1 heartbeat.
5 Breathe in through the same nostril, counting 4 heartbeats.
6 Hold the breath with full lungs, counting 16 heartbeats.

Right nostril

7 Now shift the pressure to the left nostril using the long and ring fingers, removing the thumb from the nose.
8 Breathe out calmly through the right nostril, counting 8 heartbeats.
9 Hold the breath, counting 1 heartbeat.
10 Breathe in through the same nostril, counting 4 heartbeats.
11 Hold the breath with full lungs, counting 16 heartbeats.
12 Continue as in point 3 above and repeat the pattern by alternating between the nostrils. To begin with, do 3 repetitions on each side, gradually increasing to 8 on each side.

The heartbeats can be counted by holding the left hand around the right wrist. To begin with, counting heartbeats is less important than achieving a calm, relaxed flow between the various parts of the practice, i.e., breathe out – hold – breathe in – hold – change nostril. The breathing should be neither too deep nor too superficial, and there should be no need to take in extra air through the mouth.

Joyful breathing
sukha purvak

Pump breathing

1. Lie on the back with the arms along the sides.
2. Fill the lungs by using the full yoga breathing.
3. While breathing out, bend the left leg and raise it over the chest, simultaneously lifting the head towards the knee. Link the hands around the shin and pull the leg close to the forehead. Keep the right leg slightly off the ground and push the heel away from the body with the foot flexed so that the toes point towards the body.
4. While breathing in, calmly lay the head, legs and arms down again.
5. When breathing out next time, bend up the right leg and repeat the movements.
6. Repeat 5-7 times with each leg.
7. Rest while lying on the back.

Breathe deeply and regularly during this practice. In the beginning, the practice may be repeated 5 times with each leg, alternating between them. With practice it should become possible to change legs in the air without letting them rest on the ground in between. The number of repetitions may also be increased as the abdominal muscles get stronger.

Cat breathing

1 Sit on the heels with the hands in the lap.
2 Bend forwards and place the palms on the ground. Kneel on all fours.
3 While breathing out, curve the back upwards and pull the chin towards the hollow of the throat (**PICTURE 1**). Stick the tongue out and extend it towards the chin.
4 While breathing in, curve the spine downwards so that the head and the bottom are raised (**PICTURE 2**). Roll the tongue backwards in the mouth.
5 Repeat 5-10 times with calm and regular movements that follow the breathing.
6 Sit down in the starting pose and rest.

PICTURE 1

PICTURE 2

Standing breathing

1 Stand with the arms at the sides and the legs apart. PICTURE 1

2 While breathing in, lift the arms forwards, up and out.

3 While still breathing in, stretch the arms backwards slightly so that the chest is lifted and the lungs can be completely filled with air. Do not bend the spine too far back. PICTURE 2

4 Breathe out by letting the arms and upper body fall towards the knees. PICTURE 3

5 Repeat 5-7 times.

PICTURE 1

PICTURE 3

Standing breathing

PICTURE 2

Cooling breath

sitali pranayama

1. Sit cross-legged.
2. Place the right index finger over the right nostril.
3. Roll the tongue to form a tube that protrudes slightly from the mouth, or place the tongue at the base of the front teeth and pout the lips.
4. Breathe in through the mouth so that the air flows along the tongue.
5. Breathe out through the left nostril.

The ability to shape the tongue like a tube is hereditary, not a question of training. Those who cannot do it can use the alternative method of pressing the tongue against the lower front teeth, pouting the lips and breathing in by directing the air along the tongue.

This breathing practice is said to have a cooling effect on the body. It may be continued for up to 5 minutes.

Spontaneous inhalation

1. Lie on the back or stand with the legs slightly apart.
2. Breathe slowly and forcefully out through the nose, emptying the lungs.
3. Let the breath flow in by itself.
4. Exhale forcefully a second time.
5. Again, let the air flow back into the lungs of its own accord.
6. Repeat this pattern until the body spontaneously responds by drawing a long, deep breath.
7. Then rest.

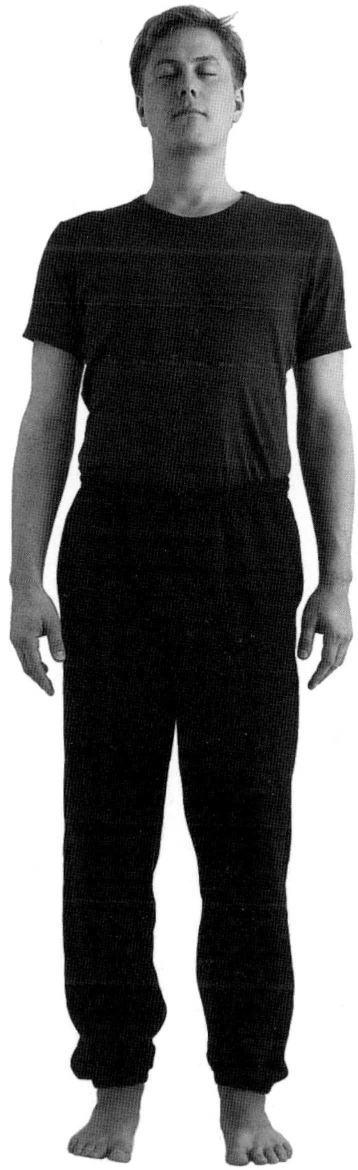

Photo: Torbjørn Hobbel

MEDITATION PRACTICES

Observing the breath

Meditation on breath

1 Sit comfortably with the legs crossed, or sit in a chair with good support to the lower back. Let the hands rest in the lap, palms up.

2 Relax the inside of the mouth: the tongue, throat, mouth and jaws.

3 Effortlessly let the attention follow the breath going in and out. Do not intentionally change the manner of breathing, just observe the air flowing in and out.

4 After 1-2 minutes, when well established in the first part of this practice (steps 1-3 above), direct the attention to the openings of the nostrils, and observe the air passing through them – in and out. At the same time, listen to the faint, almost imperceptible sound made by this flow of air.

5 Whenever the attention is derailed, for example by thoughts or images, effortlessly and gently return to observing the breath as described in point 4.

6 Continue for 5-10 minutes.

Photo: Ole Gjems-Onstad

Varieties of this practice are said to have been Buddha's preferred method of meditating. In certain contexts today, the practice is referred to as a variety of zen meditation, vipassana or mindfulness meditation.

Body feeling

Meditation on body sensations

Starting pose

Preferably, lie on the back, but sitting in a comfortable chair is an acceptable alternative. Close the eyes.

Start

Turn the attention to the whole body to become aware of any sensations, movements, pressure, tiredness, pain, twitching, movements, etc.

Light focus – observation

Effortlessly and gently watch and follow whatever attracts the attention from moment to moment (for instance, tension in the back). Be aware of what this is and observe it.

Floating focus

When using the attention in this way, do not intentionally try to change anything. If the sensations in focus increase or diminish, or even remain unchanged or move to some other location, just observe this happening. The attention should uncritically follow whatever in the body draws it at any given moment.

Let thoughts come and go

From time to time, the attention may be diverted by thoughts, feelings, images, etc. Whenever this happens, calmly and effortlessly return the attention to whatever it is that catches it at that moment. Body feeling is usually performed for 5-30 minutes, and it is all right to fall asleep during this time.

Body feeling is a kind of meditation on the body. Varieties of the practice frequently feature in zen meditation, vipassana and mindfulness meditation.

Acem Meditation

Meditation on sound

To get started in Acem Meditation, an introductory course with personal instruction is required. The practice cannot be learned from books. However, Acem Meditation is easy to learn and combines well both with yoga and an active, modern lifestyle.

Meditation sound and free mental attitude

Acem Meditation is practised while sitting comfortably in a chair or on a bed, in an environment which is quiet and free from external interference, sudden loud noises and strong light. The effects are reduced in crowded public places such as on a bus, train or aeroplane. The eyes should be closed. Without any effort or pressure, the student mentally repeats a meditation sound. Acem Meditation may be practised alone or in a group. The recommended duration and frequency is 30 minutes twice daily, or 45 minutes once a day.

Effects

Acem Meditation fosters relaxation, more energy for daily activities and, if practised regularly over time, personality development. The practice is a way of expanding one's psychological and existential freedom through deep relaxation of body and mind, and by developing a greater capacity to process present and past experiences. If practised regularly, it will contribute towards a strengthening of the inner foundations of identity, yielding benefits at work and in one's relationships to self, others and the world in general. Sporadic practice is also effective, but mostly in terms of relaxation and increased energy.

More information

Further information is available on the Internet at www.acem.com. The book *Fighting Stress* (Acem Publishing, 2008) summarizes scientific investigations into this form of meditation.

ARDEN
Photo: Karin Malmberg

Photo: Alesandro Ripellino

YOGA PROGRAMMES

The best results from yoga are obtained if there is time, interest and persistence to follow a systematic set of programmes which guide progression.

The best results from yoga are obtained by following a systematic and balanced programme with an unhurried progression. The table below gives an overview according to the various levels of challenge. In addition, suggestions for yoga training programmes are given on the following pages. Each person should find out where to start, and decide from his rate of progress how long to spend on each programme. There is no point in advancing quickly; it is better to allow oneself enough time to master each programme thoroughly.

The preliminary programmes are suited for those who have never practised yoga before or who need to loosen up tendons, muscles and joints, as well as familiarize themselves with the breathing practices.

The programmes for beginners contain easier versions of the various groups of postures.

The programmes for experienced and advanced yoga students presuppose some training and suppleness in the body, along with a mastery of the breathing practices.

Each of the programmes requires a few weeks of daily practice or a longer period of occasional practice. Several months of regular yoga practice are required for the transition from the experienced programme to the advanced programme. Subsequently, a student may want to design his own programmes to serve his needs, disposition, body condition and circumstances. The general patterns indicated below may serve as a guideline.

Every programme starts with some breathing practices. These are followed by a number of yoga postures taken from the main groups: inversion postures, backward bends, forward bends and twists. In addition, there is a group of miscellaneous optional postures to draw from. If time is limited, pick a few postures, preferably one from each of the main types in the left-hand column of the table.

All programmes should end with the corpse pose, ideally followed by some kind of meditation. Those who practise meditation regularly should do so after the corpse pose.

Main type of posture	Category			
	Preliminaries	Beginner	Experienced	Advanced
Inversion postures	Low shoulderstand	Low shoulderstand	High shoulderstand	High shoulderstand Headstand
Backward bends	Low cobra Half locust	Half cobra Half bow Half camel Bridge Half fish Half locust	High cobra Half bow Half camel Half fish Half locust	High cobra Bow Camel Locust Upward bow
Forward bends	Seated sidebend (I)	Seated sidebend (I) Dog Standing forward bend	Seated sidebend (I) Plough Standing forward bend Seated forward bend	Seated sidebend (I) & (II) Plough Standing forward bend Seated forward bend
Twists	Triangle Twist (I) Reclining twist (I)	Triangle Twist (I) Reclining twist (I)	Triangle Twist (II) Reclining twist (II)	Triangle Twist (II)
Balance postures	Tree/Balance (I)	Tree/Balance (I)	Tree/Balance (I) & (II)	Balance (II)
Combined postures		Thunder pose	Thunder pose	Thunder pose Sun salutation
Other postures	Dorsal hand hold Shoulder roll Head postures Eye practices Stomach waves	Eye practices Stomach waves	Eye practices	Abdominal lock Eye practices
Impulse practices	Impulsive slow twist (I)	Impulsive slow twist (I)	Impulsive slow twist (II)	Rapid shaking Impulsive slow twist (I) & (II)
Sitting postures	Sitting on the heels Sitting with crossed legs	Sitting on the heels Sitting with crossed legs	Sitting on the heels Sitting with crossed legs	Sitting on the heels Sitting with crossed legs Half lotus
Breathing practices	Abdominal breathing Costal breathing High costal breathing Cat breathing Standing breathing Spontaneous inhalation	Yoga breathing Joyful breathing (I) Pump breathing Cat breathing Standing breathing Spontaneous inhalation Cooling breath	Yoga breathing Joyful breathing (I) Pump breathing Spontaneous inhalation Cooling breath	Yoga breathing Joyful breathing (II) Spontaneous inhalation
Finishing	Corpse	Corpse	Corpse	Corpse
Meditations		Observing the breath 5 minutes	Body feeling 10 minutes	Acem Meditation 30 minutes

PRELIMINARIES

Target group: Those who have never done yoga regularly before or who need to loosen up their bodies. The postures marked with o are considered especially important.

Programme 1

- o Abdominal breathing x 7 — p. 122
- Spontaneous inhalation x 1 — p. 133
- Sitting on the heels — p. 118
- Dorsal hand hold — p. 100
- Shoulder roll — p. 101
- Stomach waves — p. 105
- o Low shoulderstand — p. 54
- o Triangle — p. 86
- Tree (I) — p. 90
- o Seated sidebend (I) — p. 76
- o Twist (I) — p. 82
- o Low cobra — p. 60
- o Half locust — p. 68
- Impulsive slow twist (I) — p. 108
- o Corpse — p. 114

Programme 2

- o Abdominal breathing x 7 – first week — p. 122
- Costal breathing x 7 – second week — p. 123
- High costal breathing x 7 – third week — p. 123
- Cat breathing x 4 — p. 129
- Standing breathing — p. 130
- o Triangle — p. 86
- Tree (I) — p. 90
- Dorsal hand hold — p. 100
- Head roll — p. 102
- Eye practices — p. 103
- o Low shoulderstand — p. 54
- Reclining twist (I) — p. 84
- o Low cobra — p. 60
- Sitting crossed legged — p. 118
- Impulsive slow twist (I) — p. 108
- o Corpse — p. 114

BEGINNERS

Target group: Those who have already developed a modest degree of suppleness or who are returning to yoga after a break. Postures marked with o are considered especially important. Breathing meditation may be replaced by an established meditation practice.

Programme 3

- o Full yoga breathing x 7, lying down — p. 124
- Joyful breathing (I) x 7 — p. 126
- Pump breathing x 7 — p. 128
- Cooling breath x 7 — p. 132
- Stomach waves — p. 105
- Eye practices — p. 103
- o Thunder pose — p. 94
- o Low shoulderstand — p. 54
- Bridge — p. 66
- o Seated sidebend (I) — p. 76
- Dog — p. 79
- o Twist (I) — p. 82
- o Half cobra — p. 70
- Triangle — p. 86
- Tree (II) — p. 91
- Impulsive slow twist (II) — p. 109
- o Corpse — p. 114

Observing the breath 5 minutes

— p. 136

Programme 4

- o Full yoga breathing x 7, lying down — p. 124
- Cat breathing x 7 — p. 129
- Spontaneous inhalation x 1 — p. 133
- Standing breathing x 4 — p. 130
- o Thunder pose x 2 — p. 94
- o Low shoulderstand — p. 54
- o Half fish — p. 67
- o Half locust — p. 68
- o Seated sidebend (I) — p. 76
- Dog — p. 79
- Half camel — p. 64
- o Reclining twist (I) — p. 84
- o Standing forward bend — p. 75
- Half bow — p. 62
- Impulsive slow twist (I) — p. 108
- o Corpse — p. 114

Observing the breath 5 minutes

— p. 136

EXPERIENCED

Target group: Those who have thoroughly mastered the programmes for beginners. Postures marked with o are considered especially important. Body feeling is optional, according to interest.

Programme 5

- o Full yoga breathing x 7, crossed legs — p. 124
- Joyful breathing (I) — p. 126
- Spontaneous inhalation x 1 — p. 133
- Eye practices — p. 103
- o Thunder pose x 2 — p. 94
- o High shoulderstand — p. 55
- o Seated sidebend (II) — p. 77
- o Half bow — p. 62
- o Plough — p. 78
- o High cobra — p. 61
- o Half locust — p. 68
- o Twist (II) — p. 83
- Tree (I) — p. 90
- Tree (II) — p. 91
- Impulsive slow twist (I) — p. 108
- o Corpse — p. 114

Body feeling 10 minutes
— p. 137

Programme 6

- o Full yoga breathing x 7, crossed legs — p. 124
- Pump breathing x 7 — p. 128
- Cooling breath — p. 132
- Eye practices — p. 103
- o Thunder pose x 2 — p. 94
- o High shoulderstand — p. 55
- o Half fish — p. 67
- o Standing forward bend — p. 75
- Half camel — p. 64
- Reclining twist (II) — p. 85
- o Plough — p. 78
- o High cobra — p. 61
- Triangle — p. 86
- Tree (I) — p. 90
- Half bow — p. 62
- Impulsive slow twist (I) — p. 108
- o Corpse — p. 114

Body feeling 10 minutes
— p. 137

ADVANCED

Target group: Those who have completely mastered the programmes for experienced yoga students. Postures marked with o are considered especially important. Meditations are chosen according to interest.

Programme 7

- o Full yoga breathing x 7, crossed legs — p. 124
- Joyful breathing (II) — p. 126
- Eye practices — p. 103
- Sun salutation x 6 — p. 96
- o Thunder pose x 2 — p. 94
- o Headstand or high shoulderstand — p. 56 / p. 55
- o Plough — p. 78
- o High cobra — p. 61
- o Seated sidebend (I) — p. 76
- o Twist (II) — p. 83
- o Locust — p. 69
- Triangle — p. 86
- Tree (II) — p. 91
- o Abdominal lock — p. 104
- o Seated forward bend — p. 74
- Impulsive slow twist (II) — p. 109
- o Corpse — p. 114

Observing the breath or Body feeling 10 minutes
or Acem Meditation 30 minutes
— pp. 136-138

Programme 8

- o Full yoga breathing x 7, crossed legs — p. 124
- Spontaneous inhalation x 1 — p. 133
- Sun salutation x 6 — p. 96
- o Thunder pose x 2 — p. 94
- o Headstand or high shoulderstand — p. 56 / p. 55
- o Seated sidebend (II) — p. 77
- o High cobra — p. 61
- o Locust — p. 69
- Triangle — p. 86
- Tree (II) — p. 91
- o Plough — p. 78
- Camel — p. 65
- o Twist (II) — p. 83
- o Standing forward bend — p. 75
- Upward bow or Bow — p. 71 / p. 63
- Rapid shaking — p. 110
- o Corpse — p. 114

Observing the breath or Body feeling 10 minutes
or Acem Meditation 30 minutes
— pp. 136-138

Photo: Torbjørn Hobbel

EFFECTS OF YOGA

Silence has many faces.

The stillness lingering over a lake at night.

The quiet spot at the centre of a storm.

The serenity of a loving gaze.

Silence may convey peace, calm and clarity. It may bring us face to face with who we are – for good and for bad.

We may be longing for peace but may nevertheless keep letting opportunities for silence pass by unnoticed.

To practise yoga and meditation is to get in touch with the silent undercurrents of life.

FROM STILLHETENS PSYKOLOGI
[THE PSYCHOLOGY OF SILENCE]
A BOOK ON ACEM MEDITATION

Doing yoga for 10-30 minutes or more every day provides systematic and varied training for the main groups of muscles in the body, along with the tendons and joints. Yoga loosens up some of the stiffness of the body in a slow and gentle way without pain or strain. Incrementally, the body becomes freer and more energetic; the risk of injuries is reduced. Well-being, vitality and strength are likely to increase. Yoga also improves the coordination between body, breath and mind.

Special effects?

Many yoga books claim that each posture has specific effects on the inner organs, nerve centres and hormonal glands. In this way, the postures and the breathing are supposed to alleviate various illnesses and bodily ailments. With the exception of localized musculoskeletal problems, there is hardly any scientific evidence to support such claims. However, several reliable studies show that yoga in general has a beneficial effect on the health of body and mind. We therefore take the view that the most important effects of yoga are not related to specific postures, but rather come from practising well-composed yoga programmes.

Alternating between rest and activity

Bodily training entails activation and exertion. The ability to change between different levels of activation is an advantage, permitting a person to switch easily and quickly from rest to activity and back to rest when the physical or psychological challenges have ceased. A person who is capable of such transitions at work, in leisure time and in various social contexts is less likely to suffer lasting stress than someone who activates rapidly but does not change to a lower gear when the challenge is over. Yoga involves developing the capacity to adapt swiftly to the demands of a situation, i.e., to make healthy transitions. Stressing down may reduce the risk of cardiovascular disease and strengthen the immune system to combat infections and sporadic cellular malformations that sometimes turn into cancer. Yoga modifies the autonomous system which is responsible for stress levels in the body, brain and mind.

Joy of breathing

Working with the breath trains the respiratory muscles. Some people habitually hold their breath in stressful situations, while others tend to hyperventilate. Some tighten their abdomen; others notice a pressure in their chest which may even make it hard to breathe. Changing these habits comes as a great relief. Breathing becomes associated with joy and a feeling of freedom and well-being. In addition, working with both the breathing and the body movements may increase access to emotional and cognitive resources.

Body awareness

Cultivating a free, open mental attitude significantly reduces unnecessary muscular exertions during yoga. This observant way of using the body is likely to translate into other areas of life as well, increasing one's sensitivity to the signals of one's body as well as other people's. Gradually, alternative ways of being in the body are established, and stress residuals from the day are less likely to persist.

A human being is a bit like a guitar. The mind is the strings, the body is the sounding board that gives resonance. A fine-tuned body is more sensitive to emotion, cognition and sensation. This awareness may lessen any build-up of tension. Likewise, a body with a high capacity to relax is also likely to connect to the silent impulses which may otherwise remain hidden by stress and activity. Some yoga practitioners have discovered feelings that had previously been concealed by bodily tensions. Some report an improved capacity for interpersonal understanding and intimacy, or an increased responsiveness to art and nature.

Photo: Ole Gjems-Onstad

Photo: Roland Nilsson

BREATHING AND THE MUSCLES

If the muscles are not well relaxed when breathing out, the muscle fibres tend to remain tense. The back, abdomen, pelvis and hips are likely to be affected by not relaxing fully.

Breathing is controlled by the autonomous nervous system through a reflex in the brainstem. Lower levels of oxygen in the blood stimulate the brain centre for breathing to cause the diaphragm to contract. This contraction creates a negative pressure in the chest and air is drawn into the lungs. Afterwards the diaphragm relaxes. The elasticity of the chest and the abdomen, as well as the positive pressure in the abdomen created by the inhaled air, spontaneously force the air out again.

It is preferable to exhale through the nose. When agitated, we need more ventilation and frequently open our mouths to allow in more oxygen. We draw air into the lungs to supply oxygen to all the tissues of the body. Our cells need oxygen to maintain their normal metabolism. We breathe out to get rid of carbon dioxide produced by the expenditure of energy in the cells. Carbon dioxide is transported in the blood stream from the cells to the lungs, and removed from the body when we breathe out.

Breathing – spontaneous or controlled?

We need not think about breathing in and out. Our breathing can take care of itself. But because the muscle fibres in the diaphragm are similar to our skeletal muscles, we can control our breathing. We are able to decide how we want to breathe in, hold our breath, breathe out, etc. In this way, the diaphragm is a rather unique part of the body – its movements may be governed by both unconscious and conscious mechanisms.

The diaphragm takes the form of two domes, and it divides our body into two: the chest, containing the lungs and heart, above it; the abdomen, containing the guts and other inner organs, below it. The muscular fibres of the diaphragm are attached to the lower ribs, and there is a flat tendon sheet on the top of the domes.

In the diaphragm there are rapid and slow muscle fibres which provide a wide range of options for how this muscle may work. The diaphragm has great endurance; it does not get tired as it is well supplied with blood. The main nerve that governs its action comes from a part of the brain that is closely connected to autonomic activities and our emotional life. Accordingly, it is sensitive not only to physical demands but to more subtle factors such as emotional and cognitive stress.

Photo: Roland Nilsson

Yoga and breathing may open our senses and make us more responsive to the beauty of nature. They may also increase our empathy towards others.

Psychological tensions may limit the work and the relaxation of the diaphragm. This will hamper good breathing. If the muscles are not well relaxed when breathing out, the muscle fibres tend to remain tense. The back, stomach, pelvis and hips will also be affected and will not relax fully. Over time, this may lead to bodily pain and other problems.

If the diaphragm is not contracting fully, it may have to use the auxiliary muscles in order to get enough air into the body. The auxiliary muscles are located in the chest, shoulders and neck. Normally, they are used only when we are involved in physical exertions and the body needs extra oxygen. Ideally, these auxiliary muscles should not be used in less strenuous conditions because their use stresses the body. Tensions in the diaphragm, however, may limit the free breathing of the abdomen and lower chest. Such limitations are then compensated for by extra use of the chest and neck muscles. Thus, psychological strain may render the breathing bound and tense, causing more physical stress than is necessary.

Good breathing

Good breathing makes it easier to work through difficult experiences and stress; it also facilitates the use of physical, cognitive and emotional resources. Breathing is "contagious" to those around us. A person whose abdomen moves to the rhythm of relaxed breathing and whose chest seems alive often communicates a calm that spreads to others. Likewise, a mother holding her child will often transmit her state of mind to the infant – whether relaxed or stressed - partly through her breathing, but also by the way she moves. Similarly, a teacher who is at ease may help students to focus, listen and absorb what he is saying, whereas if he is tense, he may distract them by being restless, irritable or critical.

The joy of breathing is something we can feel throughout the day: at work, when spending time with friends or loved ones, or when out walking in the countryside, in the mountains or along the shores of a river, lake or the ocean. It feels good to draw a deep breath of fresh air. The chest and the abdomen move naturally, the air flows freely in and out and vitalizes body and mind. We are in tune with nature.

Photo: Roland Nilsson

Photo: Karin Malmberg

APPENDIX

RETREAT CENTRES

At retreats, the deepening processes of meditation and yoga are facilitated by the serene environment.

Acem International Retreat Centre
Halvorsbøle, Norway

Halvorsbøle is situated one hour's drive outside Oslo. The centre stands on a hill with a panoramic view of the Randsfjord lake and nearby hamlets. The surroundings are stunningly beautiful and epitomise the deep peace and quiet of Scandinavia.

In the past, the site served as a venue for the Norwegian government's annual budget talks, as well as for the negotiations that led to the Oslo Accords between Israel and the PLO in 1993.

Halvorsbøle has access to a charming small beach. Another lake, famous for its canoeing facilities, is situated nearby. A network of narrow roads and paths in the forest makes the location ideal for walks in the summer and skiing in the winter.

Retreat participants are usually accommodated in single rooms with private bathrooms and a direct view of the lake. The Halvorsbøle cuisine is lactovegetarian, well suited for long meditations. Shared transport from Oslo Airport Gardermoen or Oslo city centre can be arranged.

Acem Nordic Retreat Centre
Lundsholm, Sweden

The Acem Nordic Retreat Centre at Lundsholm lies on a small peninsula by Mangen lake, 25 km from the town of Arvika. It is a peaceful setting remote from the hustle and bustle of modern city life.

The retreat centre is built around an old country house. A new building in traditional style and a number of charming cottages all have single rooms with private bathrooms, while the other buildings, including the main house dating back to 1850, have basic but convenient single rooms with shared bathroom. The new building has a beautiful hall for meetings and meditation.

Lundsholm offers abundant opportunities for walking, cycling, swimming and rowing, as well as skiing and sometimes skating in the winter. The area is sparsely populated, with beautiful forests and the small, red, roadside houses typical of rural Sweden. The silence is broken only by birdsong and the occasional looncall. If you are lucky, you may get a glimpse of hare, moose or deer.

RETREATS

Acem School of Meditation and Acem School of Yoga arrange a variety of retreats in Scandinavia and other parts of the world. These retreats may last for a weekend, one week and a few extend up to three weeks.

INDEX

O

P

R

S

About the authors

Are Holen (born 1945) became involved in yoga and breathing practices at the age of 16. At 17, he learnt to meditate and he has been practising ever since. His teaching of yoga and meditation has yielded valuable experiences to innumerable fellow yoga students. In Norway in 1966, he founded Acem School of Meditation, today an international organization. In 1968, he founded Acem School of Yoga.

Are Holen first qualified as a psychologist, later completing medical school. He specialized in psychiatry and worked as a psychotherapist. His principal career, however, has been in academia. He has held academic positions at the University of Oslo, Stanford University, and the University of California, San Francisco; he is currently a professor at the Norwegian University of Science and Technology. In his early twenties, he studied Sanskrit for three years. In his leisure time, he has continued to teach yoga and meditation.

Torbjørn Hobbel (born 1951) has been practising meditation and yoga since 1967. In 1975, he became an Acem Meditation initiator. In 1998, he founded Acem India. He is an adviser to Acem School of Yoga. He regularly, conducts courses and retreats in Europe and Asia.

Torbjørn Hobbel has an MA in Nordic languages and literature. In the past, he worked as a college teacher of Norwegian, history and religion. Since 1994, he has been working full time in Acem, focusing on international activities.

Acem contact info

Acem International
Internet: acem.com
Email: info.acem@acem.com
Address: PO Box 2559 Solli, NO-0202 Oslo, Norway
Telephone: +47-23118700

Acem School of Yoga
acemyoga.com

Acem India
Internet: acem.in
Email: info@acem.in